MIDNIGHT
MARAUDER

A SERIES OF WESTERN NOVELS
FEATURING THE ADVENTURES OF
JOHN CRUDDER

BOOK 1

SOMEONE WINS.
SOMEONE LOSES.
SOMEONE LIVES.
SOMEONE DIES.

ROY CLINTON

Midnight Marauder

A Series of Western Novels Featuring the Adventures of John Crudder

Book 1

Roy Clinton

Published by Top Westerns Publishing

www.TopWesterns.com

For information, contact: info@topwesterns.com

Cover and Book Design by Teresa Lauer

Edited by Sharon Smith

Printed in the United States of America

First Printing: April 2018

ISBN: 978-0-9997351-1-4

Other Books by Roy Clinton

Clint's Journey Home: A Cowboy's Guide to Hope & Freedom from Addiction

Midnight Marauder Series

Midnight Marauder, Book One

Return of Midnight Marauder, Book Two

Revenge of Midnight Marauder, Book Three

Midnight Marauder Goes Home, Book Four
Available for preorder. To be released September, 2018.

These books and others can be found on
www.TopWesterns.com and www.Amazon.com.

Dedication

This book is dedicated to my Grandchildren:

Maxwell

JD

Lincoln

Mayson

Truett

Table of Contents

PROLOGUE: 1872

L eaves rustled as the wind blew down the otherwise soundless street. John Crudder slipped from the saddle of Midnight and looped the reins over the fence at the back of the livery stable. A horse on the other side of the fence nickered a greeting to Midnight but Midnight didn't return the acknowledgment.

John glanced at the sky and confirmed dawn was still several hours away. This was the first of many planned trips back to Bandera since he gave up his job as town marshal the year before. He arrived in the wee hours of the morning so no one would know of his presence.

Crudder slipped down the alley behind Main Street,

carefully moving to not make any noise. He paused several minutes to take in the night sounds. All he heard was a coyote in the distance singing its nightly aria. John walked down the side of Davis Mercantile so he could see from one end of town to the other. All the hitching rails were empty except the one in front of the Cheer Up Saloon. The two horses left there had most likely been forgotten by their drunken owners as they slept off their stupor somewhere within the bowels of the saloon—most likely upstairs with some paid companionship.

John couldn't stand to see horses mistreated. Silently, he crept up to each of the neglected horses, released the girth, and carefully placed the saddles and blankets on the ground by the hitching rail. Both expelled air from their mouths and noses and dropped their heads to finally relax for the evening. Crudder resumed his slow move down Main Street until he got to the fancy Victorian home that stood as the centerpiece of town.

Judge Gideon Anderson liked the fact that he was often called the father of the town, a title undeserved since he neither started the town nor made any significant contribution to it. But he was revered nonetheless. As chairman of the deacon board at the church as well as the presiding officer in the court, he came in contact with many of the Bandera citizens every week. Known for his philanthropy, Judge Gideon had contributed to various causes and had helped out numerous citizens who had fallen on hard times.

No one seemed to know the source of the judge's wealth. But his stately mansion stood in the heart of town as a monument to the man most of the town admired. Little did they know that he was the mastermind behind a group of six ruthless people who were systematically robbing the town and many of its citizens. They left a trail of blood hidden by the sudden disappearances of several ranch and business owners. One by one, the abandoned ranches and businesses were bought at bargain prices by the unholy six, the town council.

The town council consisted of Mayor Farley Wright, Sally Jenson, who owned the Better Days Hotel, Betsy Hawkins, owner of the Cheer Up Saloon, Seth Davis, who owned the mercantile, and Harvey Fowler, who owned the bank. They were all equally guilty but someone had to be first.

John Crudder slipped around behind the judge's house. He placed a slim knife between the door and doorframe, flipping the latch out of the way. Cora Potter, the judge's longtime housekeeper and cook, had her bedroom just inside the door across the hall from the kitchen. John could hear her rhythmic breathing as he made his way past her half-opened door to the base of the stairs. He had never climbed the stairs when he was marshal and came to call on the judge. However, from his previous visits, Crudder knew that several of the treads would squeak for he had carefully listened to Cora as she went up and down. Carefully avoiding those steps, John climbed to the top of the stairs and paused to listen.

He could still hear Ms. Potter's breathing as he approached the judge's bedroom. John paused outside the door and listened to Judge Gideon's loud snoring. Slipping a candle from his pocket, Crudder lit it and cupped his hand around the flame to contain the light. Looking away from the flame to preserve his ability to see in the dark, he allowed the candle to burn for about a minute until it was dripping wax down all sides. He blew out the flame and quietly turned the knob of the judge's bedroom door. Carefully closing the door behind him, John stood in the shadows and allowed his eyes to adjust to the darkened room.

Prologue: 1872

Silently, John reached his left hand up his right sleeve and removed the dagger from its scabbard. Crudder approached the judge's bed and listened to the contented snoring coming from the man who had so callously cheated and robbed the citizens of Bandera, all the time being revered as a pillar of the community.

John placed the warm candle on the judge's nightstand, clamped his right hand over the judge's mouth, and then instantly placed the end of the dagger into the edge of the judge's ear.

"If you value the life of Cora Potter, you will not make a sound or move at all. If you do, I will be forced to take her life as well. This is judgment day for you. I am your judge and I will be your executioner. I am gonna remove my hand from your mouth but if you make a sound, you are deciding to end Ms. Potter's life. Do you understand?"

The judge nodded. Crudder said, "Judge, do you recognize my voice?"

The judge nodded.

"Judge Gideon, you have been found guilty of murder, theft, and numerous other crimes as you have lined your pockets and those of the other five members of the town council. You have been sentenced to death. You used your position and influence to enrich yourself and the rest of the council. Your guilt is greater than theirs. My only regret is that I can only execute you once for your crimes. Do you have anything to say before I carry out your sentence?"

Judge Gideon Anderson began to weep, and meekly said, "I never meant to hurt anybody. And I only wanted people to look up to me for all that I do for the town. I'm not really a bad man."

Crudder had heard enough. With one quick movement, he drove the dagger deep into his brain. The judge stiffened and then his body shuddered and instantly relaxed. John removed the dagger, carefully wiped it with his handkerchief, and returned it to the scabbard on his forearm. Then he picked up the candle from the judge's nightstand, removed a small amount of the warm wax, and judiciously placed it in the judge's ear. He then rearranged the judge's body so it looked like he was sleeping, gently smoothing out the sheets and blanket.

Just before he left the room, John removed his hat and bowed his head. "God, I think most people have some good in them but I have not been able to find anything in Judge Gideon's life that's commendable. Perhaps there's somethin' there I don't know about. If there is, I hope you'll consider that as you pass judgment on this earthly judge."

John left the judge's bedroom, closing the door and moving back to the staircase. He crept down the stairs, once again avoiding the squeaking treads. Passing Ms. Potter's room, he heard her contented breathing. Slipping out the door, Crudder made his way back down the alley to the back of the livery stable and mounted Midnight. He rode out of town as he had come, silently without having been seen by anyone but the judge.

Shortly after sunrise, Cora Potter knocked lightly on the judge's bedroom door. "Are you awake, Judge? Your breakfast is on the table. Don't let it get cold." There was silence on the other side of the door. "It's time to get up, Judge." Ms. Potter turned the knob and pushed the door open as she called the judge's name again. "Judge, you're gonna sleep your life away. Get up for breakfast."

She walked to the judge's bed and gently shook his shoulder. When she got no response, she placed her fingers beneath the judge's nose. As she slowly realized that he was not breathing, she sat down on the edge of the bed, and quietly sobbed for the man she had secretly loved for so many years.

CHAPTER 1: 1871

J ohn Crudder rode into Bandera midday in February. The temperature had fallen to near freezing during the night. Now with the sky filled with clouds, there had been little warming by the sun. As he rode through town, John instantly liked Bandera. There were only about two blocks of downtown, consisting primarily of a few businesses, a bank, a church, the mercantile, a hotel, a saloon, and then a big Victorian house that was set in the center of town. There was a sign in front of the house that read, *Office of Judge Gideon Anderson.*

As John made his way down Main Street, he had mixed emotions. He had hoped to find need for an attorney in town. But the more he looked, he realized it would probably be many years before a lawyer hung out a shingle in Bandera. He made his way down to the courthouse, climbed down from Midnight, and wrapped the reins around the hitching rail.

He walked into the courthouse and found a few people standing around the hall talking. John approached them and asked if anyone knew where he could find Judge Anderson. He was directed down the hall to a tall man with white hair who was talking with a younger gentleman. John removed his hat, taking in the judge's appearance while patiently waiting as they talked. He looked at his long flowing hair beneath an expensive looking black felt hat. The judge was wearing a smart suit with a vest that was festooned with a gold chain from pocket to pocket. He carried a shiny black cane with a large gold handle.

After a bit, the judge turned to John and asked, "And how may I help you, young man?" John looked down at his hat then slowly met the judge's eyes.

"Well sir, I'm an attorney and new in town. I wonder if you could tell me if there is any need for an attorney in Bandera."

The judge giggled a bit and the man he had been speaking with also laughed. "Well young man, there is a need but most people don't know the value of a good lawyer so most don't use them. We've had two or three lawyers try to make a living here but each of 'em finally gave up when they could get no clients and left town. I didn't catch your name."

"I'm John Crudder. I've been out east for my schooling and

now came here hoping to set up shop."

"Well I think you may have wasted a trip. Bandera may someday see the need for a lawyer but it'll be a long while yet. You might talk to Slim here. He probably has as much need for an attorney as anyone."

"I'm Slim Hanson. I own the H&F Ranch about ten miles south of town," Slim said as he offered his hand.

"Pleased to meet you."

"And it is good to meet you. Like the judge said, I probably use lawyers more than most people in town because of the size of my ranch. But still I only see the need for a lawyer once or twice a year. And I always just ride in to San Anton and use the firm I have always worked with. Sorry to disappoint you."

The judge and Hanson made a quick appraisal of John's appearance. He was not quite five and a half feet tall. In fact, Hanson judged him to be closer to only two or three inches over five feet. His skin was bronze from his many days in the saddle. John's clothes were dusty and rather tattered. His once black hat was well worn and covered in dust.

He carried himself like a man who was raised to have deep pride in who he was. John was a small framed man but was well built. It was obvious that he took care of his body and was not a stranger to hard work.

"Well that's all right. I've found 'bout the same thing in

most of the towns where I've stopped. Those that needed a lawyer already had two or three and didn't look like a place where I'd like to live. And towns like Bandera that seem like a place where I'd like to settle down, either didn't need a lawyer or couldn't support a second one."

"You may have come from back east but it looks like you have been in the west for a while," said Judge Gideon.

"I've been working on various cattle ranches in Colorado, New Mexico, and in the Panhandle of Texas. I didn't realize I had a talent for it but I've found I can do most things on a ranch and really enjoy the work."

"Well if it's ranch work you're interested in, that's a different story," said Slim. "I can always use another good hand on my place. Do you think you might like to work for me?"

John paused and tried to remember some of the western slang he had been hearing since disembarking from the train in Denver. "I reckon I'd like that fine. I don't have any other place to be and I've time on my hands."

"That's great. Take the main road south of town and you can't miss the H&F. It's a couple of miles out, maybe a little more. See my foreman Owen. Tell 'im I sent you out and he'll get you fixed up. If you leave now you should be there by supper time."

"Thanks, Mr. Hanson. I shor do 'preciate you givin' me a

chance."

Hanson laughed, "And I 'preciate you 'preciating me. Sounds like you have been working hard to sound more like a Texan. But I still hear a bit of eastern accent. Where did you come from, New York or Boston? I hear a bit of both in your voice."

"You're shor right. I grew up in New York City and went to school in Boston."

Laughing again, "Well you're shor welcome. And call me Slim. Everyone does."

"Okay Mr. ...er, Slim. I'll make you a good hand."

"I hope you're right John. Head on out to the ranch. I'll see you at breakfast in the morning."

With that John left the courthouse feeling a bit lighter than when he came in. He mounted Midnight and headed south in a walk. He didn't see any reason to hurry since Slim seemed to only expect him to present himself to the foreman by suppertime. As he rode, he thought about how much he already liked Bandera. He had only met two people so far but if the rest were like Slim and Judge Gideon, he knew he was going to love the town.

He pulled his jacket up around his ears to ward off a bit of the cold wind. He was hoping to get away from the cold after moving out of Boston. But he guessed that even in Texas there were bound to be some cold days. Later in the afternoon, the clouds parted and the sun brought some welcomed warmth on his back. He rode on in an easy walk and after about an hour came to a large arch above an open gate. The arch contained only the initials H&F.

John turned under the arch and made his way down the ranch road up to a large house. He could see activity along the side of the house, so he rode in that direction and saw several barns, a bunkhouse, and what appeared to be a dining hall. He dismounted Midnight and led him over to the hitching rail in front of the bunkhouse. Looping reins over the rail, he ducked under it and walked into the bunkhouse.

"Could someone tell me where I could find Owen?"

"I'm Owen. How can I help you?

"My name's John Crudder. I met Mr. Hanson in town and he said I should come see you about a job."

"He did, huh. Well I don't know if we need any more hands just now. And you don't look like you are big enough to handle a horse much less be of any use on a ranch. You ever done any ranch work before?"

"Yes, I've worked ranches in Colorado, New Mexico, and several here in Texas."

"It doesn't sound like you stay anywhere very long. How come you move around so much?" Owen asked, smiling.

"Actually, I'm a lawyer. I've been looking for a place where I could open an office."

"Did you hear that boys? This Mr. John Crudder is a lawyer. And he thinks he can make a ranch hand."

The hands who had been listening closed in around them and laughed at the idea of a big city lawyer working on the ranch. Jesse, the biggest man on the ranch, pushed John and laughed and said, "This guy's not big enough to wipe his nose by himself much less be any help on the ranch." Another cowboy pushed John back toward Jesse.

The gathered cowboys continued laughing and pushing John back and forth. Jesse got a bit full of himself and grabbed John by the collar and said, "I wonder how tough this little man is. How 'bout it, little man, how tough are you?" Jesse drew back his fist and proceeded to unleash a punch that could probably put a horse on the ground. But as he threw the punch, John ducked, stepped to the left, and as Jesse turned to see where he went, John pounded his fist into Jesse's jaw. Then he hit the big man twice in the stomach. Before he could straighten up, John landed a savage right fist on Jesse's nose. There was a loud crack as Jesse's nose gave way. The giant of a man fell backwards flat on the floor. His nose gushed blood but Jesse was out cold and didn't move.

There was utter silence from the cowboys as they took

stock of what they had just seen. Jesse had never been bested in a fight that they knew of. But today they watched the toughest man they had ever known put Jesse out without even raising a sweat. Their slack faces were trying to make sense of what they had seen. How had this man of such small stature taken on Jesse and put him in his place?

Owen was also speechless. He had seen lots of fights during his time on the H&F. And he had been in more than a few himself. But he had never seen a display of fisticuffs like he had just witnessed. He couldn't say he was happy about having his strongest hand knocked out cold. But Jesse had started it and he deserved the beating he had gotten. He also deserved the ribbing he was sure to get when others heard about the one-sided fight and of how Jesse got his nose broken.

"Like I said, I came for a job. If you've got one, I would like to work. If you don't have one, I'll be on my way."

Owen looked John up and down and then smiled. "You'll do. Move your stuff into the bunkhouse. Take any bunk that is not occupied. Supper'll be in 'bout thirty minutes. Get yourself cleaned up. Those who take supper in the dining hall haf'ta have clean hands and boots and take off their hats. Rules made by Slim."

Crudder went out to Midnight and removed his bedroll and saddlebags. As he walked back into the bunkhouse, he could hear men laughing and loudly retelling the brief fight blow by blow. Jesse had come to and stumbled out the door almost running into John. At the last minute, Jesse swayed out of the way and said, "Scuse me." Those who witnessed it laughed even louder. Several went over to John and slapped him on the back. "You're all right," said one.

Then from another fellow came, "You're gonna get along well here."

A third man asked, "Where'd you learn to fight like that?"

The hands quieted down so they could hear John's response. "I did a little boxing when I was in college." They waited for more but soon realized John had said all he was going to on the subject.

As the hands were gathering for breakfast the next morning, Slim Hanson walked into the dining hall. "I hear we had some excitement 'round here last night." No one said anything in response. He continued, "Did I hear right that several of you big strong men ganged up on someone who was smaller than you?" Everyone knew this was not the time for anyone to answer. They just needed to listen to what the ranch owner had to say. Collectively, they ducked their heads and pretended to be interested in the cooling coffee in their cups. "So Jesse, did you start this fight?"

Jesse hauled his huge frame out of his chair and stood there for a moment in silence. Both of his eyes had blackened during the night and his misshapen nose was plugged with paper. "Yes sir I did, and I'm right sorry I did." The hands all laughed in unison at the sight of this man recounting the event that had changed his appearance.

"I don't want there to be tension on this ranch that is gonna cause us problems. How about it, are we gonna have any more problems like this?" Slim asked.

"No sir, you can bet I will never pick on John again." The hands laughed again with abandon.

"How about you, John? Do you have any hard feelings toward Jesse?"

John got up and went over to Jesse and stuck out his hand. "Jesse, I'm sorry I hit you so hard. I didn't mean to hurt you so much." The hands bellowed in laughter. Several left their seats and continued laughing as they tried to contain themselves.

Jesse shook John's hand. "That's all right, Little Buddy. I shouldn't ought'a picked on you." The whole dining hall erupted into applause. Jesse smiled and playfully doubled up his fist and lightly touched John on the shoulder. John returned the soft punch to Jesse's shoulder.

From that moment on, John and Jesse were the best of friends. And anytime someone tried to pick at Jesse for being beaten up by such a small man, he would say, "You better be nice or I'm gonna tell my Little Buddy you're picking on me and he'll clean your clock.

CHAPTER 2: 1856

Johnny Crudder was the only son of railroad magnate Robert Crudder, the man who had built several railroad companies and was responsible for much of the network of railroads crawling across America. Johnny grew up in the middle of high society in New York City. He knew nothing but wealth and privilege. The Fifth Avenue mansion where he was raised had numerous servants. None of them slaves. They all had various jobs including cooking, cleaning, stable hands, landscaping and groundskeeper, and chauffeur.

He was raised mainly by his nanny Alvelda. She was also his most common playmate. His parents believed it was not healthy for him to spend much time with other boys and girls since they didn't know how they were raised and didn't know if they had any diseases. Various tutors would also spend time with Johnny each day.

Johnny was a good student who often seemed to know more than his tutors. That didn't cause him any concern, but it did cause his teachers to raise the question as to whether Johnny would be better off in an environment where he could learn more. His parents quickly enrolled him in Alexander Robertson School, known for its academics and for preparing students for the best universities. Johnny excelled at all his subjects.

Each morning, the chauffeur would drive him in the enclosed buggy to school. Although he was not the only person to come to school that way, Johnny still didn't fit in well with the other children. After all, his main playmate had always been Alvelda.

When he was twelve, his parents sent him to boarding school. John was shipped off to Georgetown Preparatory School in Washington, DC, two years younger than was typical. He had the academic background and could certainly do the work required, so his father swayed the administration with a sizable endowment check sent along with young Johnny. Away from home for the first time in his life, he cried himself to sleep most nights in those early months. He wondered why his parents didn't want him at home. Johnny couldn't understand what he had done to cause them to send him away. It is not that he missed his family that much because he seldom saw his mother and father. But he did miss Alvelda, and the other household employees.

Johnny continued to excel in his studies at Georgetown. He gave himself completely to his education. Little else held any interest for him. He didn't care about spending time with the other boys. They seemed to care about everything except their studies. What Johnny did notice was many of the students seemed to take perverse joy in picking on less fortunate students.

He watched as some of the older students would tease younger schoolboys. Johnny was sometimes the target of their pranks. Once, he woke up in the middle of the night with someone holding his mouth closed and other boys tying him tightly to his bunk. They poured a bucket of water on his bunk so it would look like he had wet his bed. He stayed in the wet sheets until morning. When he was found by the dorm chaperone, he was asked who had done that to him. Johnny refused to name anyone so he was paddled as his punishment.

Being younger than any other students caused Johnny a great deal of grief. Older students not only reveled in picking on Johnny, but students closer to Johnny's age also picked on him because he was the smallest student in school. Seldom did a week pass when Johnny was not in a fight. He always came out on the short end of the stick. Johnny didn't complain. He just accepted the fact he would be the brunt of other's jokes and that he would always be picked on.

Although Johnny could take the abuse that was heaped on him, he was especially disturbed by the injustice he saw being perpetrated on other students. It always bothered him when he saw someone being mistreated who couldn't defend himself. Several times he would step into those situations only to end up being the new target of their abuse. Johnny couldn't defend himself and didn't think it was possible to keep bullies from hurting him.

Some of the injustice he saw was at the hands of teachers. He witnessed physical abuse by one of the teachers. There was even a janitor who would sexually abuse the younger boys. Johnny knew about that first hand because that same man tried to abuse him. Johnny fought and was successful in keeping the man off him but he knew several of the younger boys were nightly targets.

Johnny continued crying himself to sleep most nights. He longed for home and for being able to spend time with Alvelda and the other servants in his household. His days were spent studying and wishing he was back in New York City.

Johnny found some joy in helping other students with their studies. It soon became known that Johnny was at the top of each course of study. Students sought him out for tutoring. Although they offered him money, Johnny didn't need it, so he tutored them for free.

One day Johnny found out the school had an equestrian club. He made his way to the barn on the edge of campus and was delighted to find several additional barns filled with sleek looking horses. He had never been on horseback since he was always chauffeured in a buggy. The first time he climbed into a saddle, he was a bit frightened because of the size of the horse but he instantly fell in love with horses and riding.

Every afternoon after class Johnny would spend a couple of hours tutoring other students and then head to the stables. He not only enjoyed riding but he also enjoyed everything to do with horses. The stable hands were amused when Johnny asked if he could help them muck out the stalls. They were only too happy to share their work with him. While Johnny took joy in the work, he also learned a lot about horses. It was as if he was making up for lost time since at age twelve he had just discovered one of the greatest sources of joy he had ever known.

The first telegram Johnny sent home was to ask his father if he would buy him a horse. His father agreed and had one of his employees travel to Washington, purchase a horse for Johnny, and deliver it to Georgetown. When the horse arrived, Johnny was overwhelmed. He looked at the beautiful chestnut horse and said, "I'm going to name you Flame." His real love affair with horses was born that day.

Johnny loved riding and jumping. With his light frame, he found that he could get Flame to jump fences other horses with heavier riders would not jump. After an afternoon of riding, Johnny would go back to the stables and spend the next hour or more grooming Flame. He would carefully pick the gelding's hoofs. Then he would get the currycomb and loosen mud and dirt and any loose hair. Johnny would then take his dandy brush to get rid of the dirt and hair that the currycomb loosened. Finally, he would use a body brush to complete the process. Johnny would then spend time combing out tangles in the horse's mane and tail. Flame would neigh and Johnny would speak softly to his new friend.

While Johnny took solace spending his time with Flame, he couldn't get away from things that bothered him like watching boys being picked on by those who were older and bigger. Johnny found out the school also had a boxing club. Although he didn't know anything about boxing, Johnny wanted to learn the art of self-defense. His father had never taught him to defend himself from bullies. There had not been any instances in his life in New York City where Johnny was bullied or saw anyone being bullied.

Chapter 2: 1856

When he showed up at the gym and asked how he could join the boxing club, the boys gathered there laughed like they had just heard a funny joke. One of the older boys told Johnny with a smile, "We all fight in our own weight class. The problem is there is no one in your class. We don't have anyone that light." What Johnny appreciated was that the boy didn't ridicule him for wanting to join the team but just talked to him about the difficulties he would face. "But you can still join up. We're glad to have you."

That day, Johnny began learning the manly art of self-defense. As with every subject Johnny tackled, he was obsessed with being the best. Before long the older boys were challenging him to bouts. Johnny would take on all comers and typically win more matches than he lost. At competitions, Johnny was always the lightest boxer and he always won in his weight class. At most of the competitions, the other schools would allow him to fight in a higher weight class and almost always, Johnny would walk away the victor.

Over the next year, Johnny didn't grow much taller and continued to be the lightest member of the boxing team. But he also put on a significant amount of muscle. He perfected his technique and by the start of his second year at Georgetown, he was considered one of the best boxers on the team. He would frequently take on the older and larger members of the team to experience a challenge.

For the first time in his life, Johnny made friends with other boys. Since he was the youngest boy at school, all his friends were older. But it didn't matter to Johnny; he was glad to be welcomed as an equal. One of the things he found surprising was that several older members of the boxing team seemed to look out for Johnny the way they would for a younger brother. In those friendships, Johnny started picking up pointers on self-defense when he was not in the boxing ring. He found that there were additional things he could do to protect himself beyond what he learned from boxing. He also found that without the constraints of the rules of the boxing ring, he could find ways to equalize things when dealing with a stronger and bigger opponent.

In the spring of his second year at Georgetown, Johnny witnessed a boy being beaten up by several of the tougher boys in school. He watched as the boys, one after the other punched him in the face and then kicked him when he fell down. Johnny couldn't watch and remain uninvolved. He approached the boys and said, "Why don't you pick on someone who can fight you back?"

The boys laughed as they abandoned thoughts of stomping the unfortunate student they had been beating. The three of them turned to Johnny and said, "You are going to wish you hadn't've butted in to what doesn't concern you." The largest boy took a wild and angry rounded punch. Johnny easily sidestepped and landed three quick punches on the boy's jaw. At the same time, he pivoted his focus on the remaining boys. Both of them took swings at Johnny. But, they were no match for Johnny's quick moves and lightning-fast fists. Within a few seconds, all three boys lay in a heap, all with bloodied noses and busted lips. Johnny was not even winded.

He didn't realize that the headmaster had witnessed the fight. Johnny was called into his office to give an account of his actions. "What do you have to say for yourself, young man?" Johnny stood with his head down and tried to think of an appropriate response. He knew fighting was strictly prohibited and was grounds for expulsion.

Johnny was awash with fear as he anticipated the confrontation that would happen when his father found out he was kicked out of school for fighting. The headmaster said, "Johnny, I have had my eye on you since you got here last year. As you know, your father is a great supporter of our school. I have hoped you would behave yourself while you are here. You are a good student and have excelled on the boxing team. Why would you get into a fight in the school yard? You are not that kind of boy."

Johnny slowly raised his head and looked at the headmaster

in the eye. "Sir, I know I am not supposed to fight but I couldn't stand by and watch another boy get beaten up by a gang. I had to step in."

The headmaster listened and pursed his lips. When Johnny finished his explanation, the headmaster said, "Johnny, I still don't like fighting and I hope you will stay out of fights in the future. But, your courage in defending another student who was being abused by bullies is in keeping with the highest character traits that we exemplify at Georgetown. I want to shake your hand and congratulate you on a job well done. Those boys deserved what they got from you, and they will deserve being expelled by me. Johnny, carry on."

CHAPTER 3: 1871

L ife on the H&F was better than John could have hoped. He had never worked on such a large ranch. They said the ranch was one hundred ten sections in total. It was nearly twenty-five miles from end to end stretching across two Texas counties. It would take a cowboy on a good horse the better part of a week just to see the entire ranch.

The ranch had everything that was needed for a successful cattle operation. There were barns and line shacks scattered throughout the acreage. There were pastures for growing hay that was cut each summer and stored to feed the cattle during the winter. The Medina River ran through the ranch, along with several small lakes and wells that supplied all the water needed for the cattle and crops. The ranch raised all the produce needed to feed the hands.

About seventy-five men were on the ranch payroll. That made it the largest employer by far in Bandera and Medina counties. For the most part, the men were all well behaved. They didn't cause much trouble, even when they went to town on Saturday evening. It was understood that if they wanted to keep their jobs on the H&F, they had to behave even when they were off duty. Any fighting that was done was between themselves and done on the ranch. There were almost always brief skirmishes that didn't amount to much of anything.

The other hands immediately accepted John. It was as though he had worked on the ranch for years. He and Jesse were constant companions. They worked together and when they were not working, they hung around together. For John, Jesse became the brother he never had. And for Jesse, John was a truer friend than he had ever known. After supper, most nights, the pair could be seen walking to the bunkhouse with Jesse's big hand resting on John's little shoulders.

At the end of February, the hands spent a couple of weeks moving all the breed cows up to the fenced in acreage near the ranch headquarters. Calving would commence with the first signs of spring. For John and Jesse, that meant long days starting down near Hondo and rounding up the cows that would soon give birth. Jesse had three additional hands helping them. He was a natural cow man. Having grown up on a ranch, he had forgotten more about ranching than most other men knew.

The sign that rustlers had been in the area was noticed on the first day of the round up. Jesse spotted remnants of a camp fire. On closer inspection, he found a running iron that had been left behind by the campers in their haste to move on. "Little Buddy, come look at this."

"What's that, Jesse?" John asked as Jesse held the branding iron in the air.

"This is a runnin' iron. Rustlers use it to change the brands on cattle they steal. Haven't you ever seen one of these before?"

"I've heard tell of 'em but I've never seen one."

"The ashes are still warm. Looks like they pulled out sometime this morning. Little Buddy, I need you to ride back to headquarters and tell Owen what we found. He'll probably want to get some more men up here to go after the rustlers."

"Do you want me to go on to town and get the marshal?"

"That's up to Owen. Right now, I just need you to ride like the wind and tell Owen what we've found. My guess is he'll not mess with getting the marshal. There is not much the marshal can do until we find the rustlers. It's up to us to get our cattle back and stop these vultures before they strike again. If you ride hard, you can make headquarters by dusk. Be sure to bring back help—we're gonna need it."

And with that John mounted Midnight and headed north. He rode as fast as he dared without pushing Midnight too hard. But it seemed the faster he rode, the faster Midnight wanted to go. He gave him his head and the big black stallion streaked toward headquarters.

Less than two hours later, John Crudder arrived at headquarters. Midnight wasn't even winded. He led the great horse over to the watering trough.

"Where's Owen?" John shouted.

"He's over at Slim's house," replied one of the hands who was repairing fence to hold the breed cows when they were rounded up.

John ran to the large stone house, was up the steps and onto the porch as he yelled for Slim. Without waiting for an invitation, John ran through the opened door and yelled, "Rustlers!"

Owen and Slim came rushing from the back of the house.

"Where are they?" asked Slim.

"Jesse found their fire and a runnin' iron near Hondo," responded John.

"Mount up!" yelled Owen.

"I'm going with you," said Slim.

There were only two other hands at headquarters. Everyone

mounted up and started south toward Hondo.

"Cody," Owen shouted. "You head over toward the eastern line shack. Send everyone you pass down to Hondo. Then you high tail it down there. Gus, you get over to Tarpley. Tell everyone you see to make for Hondo, pronto. And if you see any hands on the Jay Bar, tell 'em to come join us. If we are gettin' our cattle stolen, it is only a matter of time before they get the Jay Bar cattle, too."

The riders split up. Owen, Slim, and John continued south. John gave Midnight his head again and soon Owen and Slim were so far behind that John lost sight of them. He reasoned that he would do the most good getting back to help Jesse as soon as possible.

When John got to the remains of the rustler's campfire, he found a note left by Jesse that said they were tracking the rustlers east toward San Antonio. In less than an hour, John caught up with Jesse and the rest.

"Hey Little Buddy, you made good time. I didn't expect to see you until tomorrow. Where are the others?"

"They're coming, Jesse. Owen and Slim are behind me. Owen sent Cody out east and told Gus to go to Tarpley. He also told him to roust out the Jay Bar hands."

John settled into a slower lope beside Jesse. Midnight still was not showing signs of being tired. John marveled at the stamina of the black stallion. As they rode, they continued watching the ground looking for a sign. The rustlers were not hard to follow. There were many tracks from the cattle. Jesse estimated that they got away with one to two hundred head. They had identified tracks of at least a dozen horses but Jesse said it was hard to tell for certain. He said there may be more.

"I'll bet they are hoping to get to San Anton to sell 'em to a larger outfit," said Jesse. "It wouldn't surprise me to find out they have been stealin' cattle from us all winter. If they have, we're likely to run into what they have already stolen. But that means we'll also meet up with the rest of that outlaw bunch. I shor hope Cody and Gus are able to get more help here soon. We're gonna need 'em."

The sun would soon be down. John knew they would have to make camp shortly. He hoped Owen and Slim would catch up soon.

Finally Jesse decided they had better stop for the evening. He knew the rest of the hands would keep coming until they caught up. He gave orders to build their campfire much larger than normal. He wanted the reinforcements to be able to find them easily. But the risk was they would tip their hand to the rustlers. Jesse figured it was worth the risk. They couldn't handle the rustlers by themselves so they had to leave a good signal for the rest of the hands.

Owen and Slim rode up as Jesse and John were gathering wood for the fire. Their horses were exhausted. Fortunately, they were able to make camp by a little stream. It would not be much use to a herd of cattle but it was plenty for their fatigued horses.

They made coffee and dinner consisting of beans and bacon. As they were finishing eating, Cody and the men working the eastern part of the ranch arrived. Besides the six H&F hands Gus brought, there were four riders from the Jay Bar. Within an hour, Cody and the Tarpley bunch arrived. John did a quick count and realized they had fifteen more riders. He hoped that would be enough to take on the rustlers and get their cattle back.

While John was proficient with a six-shooter, he had never had to pull his gun on a man. He thought he could, but had never been put to the test. Sitting around the fire, he realized although there was a lot of laughing and kidding going on, tension was high. John didn't feel like joining in the banter. He moved back out of the circle over to where he had Midnight grazing. The rest of the horses were hobbled to keep them from running off, but he knew he didn't need to do anything to Midnight to keep him nearby. Midnight wanted to be wherever John was and wouldn't go anywhere without him.

John pulled a brush from his saddlebag and began to groom

his tall horse. As always, it was as though Midnight's neighs were vocalizing a "thank you" to John. As he brushed him, John spoke gently to the big thoroughbred. He realized he got as much out of the grooming as did his horse. For John, this was a time to relax and meditate, thinking back over the day, how fast Midnight had run and his boundless energy. But this was also a time for John to contemplate the fight waiting for them the next day.

Could John go up against another man? He had done so several times with his fists. If someone threatened him, he had no trouble defending himself. But pulling a gun on a man was another matter. Could he do that if he didn't have another way out? He thought he could. While he knew he couldn't do it if he was not provoked, he felt sure he could shoot another man if it was to save his life or the life of someone else.

John leaned against his upturned saddle, lowered his hat over his eyes to block out the light from the fire, and closed his eyes. Try as he might, he was not able to drift off to sleep. He kept thinking about gun fighting and wondered if he was up to the task.

In the wee hours of the morning, John heard someone moving slowly through the grass on the other side of the fire. He didn't move but just listened figuring it was probably just one of the men getting up to relieve himself. The closer he listened the more he realized others were moving around as well. John slowly got up, retrieved his saddle gun, and slipped into the shadows.

John realized the rustlers had seen their large campfire and were going to ambush them. As he waited, he counted ten men creeping in toward his friends. He was not sure what to do. Should he start shooting? Should he just wait and see what the rustlers did next? Maybe they were only going to try to scare the men and send them back to the H&F. But, that didn't make sense, he thought. They were intent on harm and he couldn't allow that.

As John took in the sight, he realized the rustlers had their six-guns out. Finally he decided to shout and wake the others up, "Hey, get up!"

At the same time he leveled his saddle gun at the three men closest to the sleeping hands. In less than a second, John had dispatched all three. As the men were falling lifelessly to the ground, the sleeping cowboys were instantly awake and firing on their attackers. John's initial shout had made him a target. In the next few seconds he was catching fire from every direction. Dropping to the ground and rolling, John came up firing as quickly as he could cock his rifle. When it was empty, he pulled his six-gun and started firing. He didn't have to aim. It was as though his gun took over his hand. All those hours of target practice were paying off.

One by one, the outlaws were dropping. John knew he had hit at least six of the rustlers. He didn't know where he hit them, only that they went down. He also knew his six-gun was empty.

Then there was silence. The rustlers lay silently on the ground. The H&F hands were spreading out to make sure there were no more threats. As he walked toward the campfire, a lone gunman came out from behind a tree and leveled his gun at Jesse.

"Jesse, watch out!" shouted John.

Jesse turned toward the threatening man but had no gun in his hand. In a split second, John pulled a dagger from the scabbard in his sleeve and in one fluid motion hurled the blade toward the outlaw. It buried itself to the hilt in the attacking man's neck. He fell without a sound.

All eyes turned to John. "Little Buddy! How did you do that?" asked Jesse.

The hands gathered around John and began slapping him on the back. "Wow! You're a one-man army!" shouted one man.

Another said, "Did you see him throw that knife?"

Owen walked among the fallen outlaws realizing that most of them had been killed by John, the little man who came to town wanting to open a law office. No one had ever seen anyone fight like John Crudder. He was indeed a one-man army.

When morning came, it didn't take the men long to round up the stolen cattle. They found more than three hundred head. And sure enough most were H&F cattle, with some from the Jay Bar. They slowly made their way back toward Bandera. In a couple of days they had the cattle back where they belonged. By the weekend, the word of John's exploits had spread all over Bandera.

On Sunday, Jesse and John mounted up and decided to go to church. Jesse said it just made sense to acknowledge their Creator after they had come so close to meeting him a few days before. When they got to town, everyone they passed lifted their hands and their voices and said, "Howdy John. Howdy Jesse." It seemed that everyone knew John now. He found it unsettling to be the center of attention. All he had intended to do was to help protect the men from outlaws.

In church, everyone was aware of the presence of Jesse and John. They looked like an odd couple sitting on the pew: Jesse, clearly the biggest man in the room, and John, just as certainly the smallest—at least in stature.

When the parson began his message, he said, "Today, we are honored to have a true hero in our midst. John Crudder almost singlehandedly wiped out a gang of rustlers that has been plaguing our county for a number of years."

John's face burned as if on fire. He knew he was turning red. He wished he could crawl out of the church without anyone seeing him.

Jesse said, "You've got that right, preacher. My Little Buddy here done saved the bunch of us. If it wasn't for him, our whole group would have been wiped out. And one of the rustlers had me dead to rights and would have killed me shor, if John hadn't got him with his knife. He threw his knife quicker than the other man could shoot. You shoulda seen it. He got him in the neck and dropped him like a rock."

A collective gasp came from the women present. The men had a smirk of admiration on their faces. Little children cried. The older boys "whooped" loudly. The parson did his best to restore order but there was nothing but pandemonium.

John got up and fled down the aisle. Jesse followed him out of the church and closed the door. "Gee Little Buddy, did I hurt your feelin's? I didn't mean to. I just wanted people to know what a great thing you did for me."

"It's not your fault, Jesse," said John. "I just don't like all of the attention. Anyone would have done what I did."

"That's just it, Little Buddy. Nobody else *could* do what you did. I've never seen anyone shoot like you did. And I shor never saw no one throw a knife like that. I didn't even know you carried a knife. And it looked like you pulled it out of your shirt.

How did you do that?"

John slowed as he walked down the street and headed toward the saloon. When they got to the boardwalk, John took a seat on the bench in front of the saloon, as Jesse plopped down next to him.

"I saw a knife throwing demonstration in Willow Springs, New Mexico, a few months ago. I was fascinated by the accuracy and speed with which a knife could be thrown. I noticed the knife thrower had a scabbard on his forearm. It just made sense to me that keeping it there was a way of having it close at hand if it was needed. I bought me a dagger just like the one I saw demonstrated. Every evening I would practice throwin' it until I got good. But Jesse, I never dreamed I would have to throw it at a man. I just thought it would be a fun pastime for me."

"I'm glad you learned to throw. And I'm glad you throwed it when you did. You saved my life, Little Buddy. Ain't nobody ever saved my life before."

They got up and walked into the saloon. As they got to the bar, they saw several hands from the H&F. They cheered in unison as they saw John Crudder. John felt his face flush again. Jesse ordered beer for the two of them.

Men gathered near John hoping to hear him tell of the gunfight. They were disappointed John didn't want the spotlight, but several who had seen the fight and several who had only heard about it started retelling the tale. With each retelling, it seemed that the story got bigger and bigger. In one version, John had a six-gun in each hand. In another, John was said to have fired a rifle from each hand. In yet another, John was flinging knives and shooting, felling the whole outlaw gang before anyone else could get off a shot.

John had a couple of swallows of his beer and turned to leave the saloon. Jesse was right with him. It seemed John and Jesse didn't need to talk. It was as if they read each other's minds. They mounted up and rode in silence back to the ranch in an easy lope

CHAPTER 4: 1861

Robert Crudder was a self-made man. He built his railroad empire from nothing and now was one of the wealthiest men in the country. His dream was for his son Johnny to someday take over the reins of leadership and continue growing his railroad empire. For Johnny to out stride his father, Robert knew he would have to have the finest education available. And for Robert, that meant one thing—Harvard University.

John shed his diminutive moniker when he arrived at Harvard at the tender age of fifteen. Although he was used to being younger than anyone else in school, he was surprised at how easily he fit in at Harvard. His time at Georgetown Prep accounted for his easy transition. In his three years at Georgetown, he had made perfect marks in each of his courses.

In his last year the teachers realized regardless of how advanced their teaching, Johnny had studied far beyond what they were teaching.

The headmaster had the faculty prepare a series of tests for Johnny to see which courses he should take. To their mild surprise, Johnny made top marks on every exam they gave. It soon became apparent they had given him all the school had to offer. It was time for him to move on to a university. When they asked him where he wanted to attend he just said one word: Harvard!

Life at Harvard was different only in that the campus was larger. John found the course work more challenging but nothing he couldn't handle. He welcomed the greater challenge for he felt he had not been living up to his full potential at Georgetown. He liked studying but especially enjoyed being pitted against other young men who represented the sharpest minds in the country. Johnny made a few friends. It seems his time at Georgetown had also made him more social. He was still the youngest student there, or at least among the youngest. But he had learned to fit in with those who were older than he was. He simply was mature beyond his years.

John was thrilled to find Harvard also had boxing and equestrian teams. He joined both and continued to gain proficiency in the sports. John found riding was natural for him.

He had a way of communicating with his mount that allowed both horse and rider to move as a unit. When he moved from Georgetown, John had reluctantly deeded Flame to the school so the horse could continue to benefit the equestrian team. He was content at Harvard to ride one of the school's horses.

On the boxing team, his prowess with his fists soon became legendary on campus. His record from Georgetown gained him immediate acceptance with the team. At each match, John emerged a winner.

In his second semester at Harvard, he discovered there were a few other students his age. He became roommates with a student his same age from a wealthy family in Philadelphia. Harrison Gray, Harry to his friends, became a trusted comrade. It was a friendship that was destined to last a lifetime, even though they would be separated by distance for much of their lives.

The Civil War was just beginning when John got to Harvard. He was well below the age of conscription. Robert Crudder thought it best to make sure his son's college years were not interrupted so he paid for a substitute to get conscripted in John's place, even though John would not be eligible for more than four years. This was a common practice. So, common in fact that of the nearly 169,000 men drafted for the Union, nearly 118,000 of them were substitutes.

John's years at Harvard seemed to fly by. He was getting a classical education. He continued the language studies he began at Georgetown. He was fluent in both Latin and Greek. John was able to master any subject placed before him. He wasn't sure what he was learning would help in his father's company but he knew his father was convinced he needed to learn as much about the world as possible. John studied literature and philosophy. He also found he had a head for higher mathematics. Young Crudder also tackled physics and chemistry.

He was not in a hurry to graduate. Indeed, he could have completed his course work one to two years before he did. But John wanted to learn everything he could while at Harvard. He was committed to stay there for a full four years.

Throughout his time at Harvard, John continued to be concerned when he saw what he felt was an injustice. There were a few bullies on campus. More than once, John used his boxing ability to defend fellow students who were the focus of a bully's rage. Even though John's reputation with his fists was well known, there always seemed to be someone who couldn't believe such a small fellow could do what they said he had done. John walked away from every fight he could, but found there were some boys who wouldn't allow that. In those cases, John made quick work of them. Usually before the bully could draw back a fist, John had dispatched him with a flurry of punches.

One of the inequities John sought to address was the fact that some students, though brilliant, had very limited financial resources. John used money from his trust fund to help students who were struggling financially. He telegraphed his father to see if he would support that effort. His father responded with a resounding "yes." Then he said something in the telegram he had never spoken in person to his son. He said, "John, I'm proud of you. I love you, son."

As John read the words, he was stunned. His father had always seemed so cold to him. Big tears appeared in his eyes. He expected his father to be against John giving money to others. From what John had seen, he was sure his father was only concerned for himself and for amassing as great a fortune as possible. Maybe John had misjudged him. And if he was wrong about his father, he wondered what else he could be wrong about.

When John was nineteen, he was called to the office of the president of the university. John immediately thought it was because some bully complained about getting his comeuppance from the diminutive boxer. As he waited outside the president's office, he had a strong feeling he would be leaving Harvard that day.

The long-faced president called John into his office. "John,

I'm afraid I have some bad news for you. Your father and mother were killed yesterday in a buggy accident. It seems that an approaching fire engine spooked one of their horses. Their buggy overturned and your parents were thrown into the path of the fire engine. The one thing to be said is that death came quickly for both of them. John, I'm sorry."

John stared ahead without uttering a sound. He was stunned. He considered his father larger than life. He never gave thought that his parents would die. He thought his father was too strong, too successful, maybe even too rich to die. But as John reflected on what he heard, he realized his parents were mortal and death comes to all.

"John, I know you want to get started home just as soon as possible. I've been checking with your professors and have found you have already far exceeded the requirements for graduation. I have taken the liberty of having your diploma prepared. Here, John," said the president as he handed him the diploma. "Congratulations on your graduation from Harvard University. I confer upon you the General Degree Diploma. May you enjoy every success in life. And may your current sorrow not alter the course of your life."

With that, John walked out of the president's office and walked across campus to his dorm. Harry was in the room studying. John told him what he had just found out and told him he was leaving Harvard. Harry wiped tears from his eyes and hugged John. With the embrace, John began to weep. At first, it was silent sobs then the sobs gave way to deep, guttural wailing. After a few moments, John composed himself, released Harry, and wiped his eyes.

"Harry, I'll say good bye for now. But I want to keep in contact with you. I know I can reach you here or through your parents in Philadelphia. You can reach me through my father's company in New York. I have to go back there and see what is needed. I'm not sure what's going to happen. All I know is I will not be coming back. The president gave me my diploma so I can just concentrate on taking care of what I can only imagine will be many loose ends."

CHAPTER 5: 1871

J ohn Crudder never sought the limelight. In fact due to his small stature, he would have much preferred to blend in. But he usually stood out and was an object of ridicule and scorn. The fame he now enjoyed for defeating the band of rustlers was certainly better than being mocked because of his size, but he still didn't like being the focus of attention.

One thing he did enjoy was having the respect of the hands. Since finding out John was a formidable fighter, the hands seemed to afford him greater deference. Some even seemed to admire him. John was completely unaccustomed to that for he had never been esteemed by others.

About a week after the encounter with the cattle thieves, Slim's daughter Charlotte happened to be just ahead of him in the chow line for breakfast. She looked to be about seventeen or eighteen years old but John couldn't be sure. Her hair was a reddish blond and her face was covered in freckles. She turned and smiled at John and John realized he had been staring. He tried to look away before she caught him but it was too late. Her blue eyes flashed and the corners of her mouth turned up in a grin.

"Hello, I'm Charlotte Hanson."

John then realized that he had been wearing his hat in the dining hall, which was against the rules. He grabbed his hat from his head and said, "Howdey Ma'am. I'm John Crudder." He rolled the brim of his hat in his hands and tried desperately to find something else to say. But he just stood there awkwardly and then looked down at his boots.

"I know who you are, Mr. Crudder. And you don't have to be so formal as to call me ma'am. Just call me Charlotte."

"All right Ma' . . . I mean Charlotte. And nobody calls me Mr. I'm just plain John."

"John, yes, but not plain by any measure. I heard how you saved the men from the rustlers. My own father said he might have been killed if it hadn't been for you."

John looked back at his boots and tried to think of an appropriate response. Nothing came to him. Finally, Charlotte said, "There is a dance tomorrow evening at the church in town.

I think my father would let me go with you if you would ask him."

This was a moment John had often dreamed about. He had never had any interaction with girls. All of his time at Georgetown, Harvard, and later in Europe had been spent with boys. John found he couldn't speak. He couldn't even look at Charlotte. Although he never had considered himself to be shy, he had to admit he never had conversations with any girl, except Alvelda's daughter and he considered her more of a sister.

Charlotte giggled and said, "That is if you want to take me to the dance. You do want to take me, don't you?"

John just nodded. "All right then it's settled. You ask my father if you can take me and then I'll be ready right after work tomorrow."

John nodded again. Charlotte's giggle turned into a laugh. But it was different from the ridiculing laughs he used to get from boys at school. Her laugh was delightful. As she chuckled, her eyes sparkled. John felt his face warm and he knew he must have been blushing.

John and Charlotte both got their breakfast. Charlotte went to the table where her father was sitting and John joined a table with some of the other hands. As he walked to his table, he turned to see where Charlotte was sitting and found Slim was staring hard at him. Charlotte was still smiling. John hurriedly turned away and took a seat beside Jesse.

Evidently the men at the table had missed his conversation with Charlotte, otherwise they would have been ribbing him. John ate quietly and never took his eyes from his plate.

"What's a matter with you, Little Buddy? You sick or somethin'?"

"No I'm fine, just thinking about things. Wondering where we're going to be working today."

"Well I can tell you that," said Jesse. "You and I are going back down south to gather up some more of the breed cows. We won't be back until tomorrow evenin'."

John groaned and dropped his head.

"Little Buddy, you're worrying me. Are you shor you're all right?"

After another minute of silence, John turned to Jesse and said, "Charlotte is expecting me to take her to a dance in town tomorrow. First I have to ask her father for permission. I was gonna work up my nerve and ask him tonight. But we're not goin' to be back here tonight."

"Well Little Buddy, it looks like now is the time to do the asking. Slim's looking right at you anyway. Why don't you go on over and ask him now?"

John swallowed hard and started to get up from the bench. What would he say to the owner of the ranch? How could he ask for a date with his daughter? He had never even been on a date. He slowly walked to the table where Slim and Charlotte were sitting. Both were staring at him. John looked at the floor as he walked. He felt like he was walking to the gallows and was getting ready to meet his executioner. Finally, he reached the table.

"Pardon me, Sir, for interrupting. Could I have a word with you?"

Slim looked him in the eye. "Sure can. What's on your mind, son?"

"Well sir, I heard there's a dance in town tomorrow night. It's not one of those dance hall kind of dances but a dance the church is puttin' on. And I was sort'a thinkin' I would like to go. I've never been to a dance before and I thought it might be kind of interesting. So I was wonderin' . . . I was thinkin' . . . What I'm tryin' to say . . ."

"Son, you don't need my permission to go to the dance. If you want to go, then by all means you should go," Slim said as he shared a smile with Charlotte. John summoned his courage, took a step toward Slim, and blurted out, "Well you see, Sir, that's the thing. I would like to go and I was wonderin' if you would mind if I were to ask Charlotte to go with me?"

Charlotte smiled and looked with anticipation at her father. Slim made a frown and looked down. John didn't think that was a good sign. He was probably going to be told he had no business taking his daughter on a date.

Slim looked up and said, "John, I would be proud for you to accompany my daughter to the dance. Come by tomorrow afternoon and I'll let you use the buggy. I want you to go straight there and then get her home at a decent hour. And I don't mean in the middle of the night. Do you think you can do that?"

John's face brightened. "Yes Sir, I can do that." John turned to leave.

"But John, aren't you forgettin' somethin'?" asked Slim.

"I don't think so, Sir."

"Well don't you think you need to ask Charlotte an' see if she wants to go with you?" Slim asked this as Charlotte beamed her brightest smile at John.

"Miss Charlotte, I would like to ask if I could accompany you . . . I mean if you could accompany me . . . Well, would you like to go to the dance with me tomorrow night?"

"Yes, Mr. Crudder, I would be pleased to go to the dance with you," replied Charlotte.

"And John one more thing," offered Slim. "Make sure you pull off work early enough tomorrow so that you can get cleaned up. Jesse can handle things after you're gone. I don't want my daughter goin' to town with you smellin' of cow poop."

John nodded and said, "Yes Sir Slim, I'll be sure to get cleaned up before I pick up your daughter."

John walked back over to Jesse. "How'd it go?" asked Jesse.

"All right I think," said John. "I think I've got a date for tomorrow night."

"Good for you, Little Buddy." Jesse slapped John's back. "I knew ya could do it. I'm proud of ya."

All of a sudden, John dropped his head and let out a soft moan.

"What's the matter now, Little Buddy?"

John groaned. "I'm going to the dance all right but the thing is, I don't know how to dance. I've never been to a dance in my life and don't know the first thing about what I'm supposed to do."

"Don't worry none about it, Little Buddy. By the time you get to the dance tomorrow night, I'll make sure you're the best dancer there. You're gonna be taught by the best dance teacher there ever was. Me! I'll have you dancin' and you'll be just fine."

Jesse and John finished breakfast and walked out of the dining hall. As he was walking through the door, John turned back to steal a look at Charlotte. She was watching him and gave him a little wave of her hand. John felt his face flush again and walked on out the door.

He followed Jesse to the corral where they saddled their horses and headed down south in a canter. After a few miles, they slowed their horses to a trot. Jesse said, "Wha'cha got on your mind, Little Buddy?"

"Jesse, I wouldn't tell anybody else this but you. But I'm more afraid of being alone with Charlotte and takin' her to the dance than I was of facin' off with the rustlers."

Jesse laughed and said, "Little Buddy, that's just natur'l. You ain't never been with a girl before so you don't know what to 'spect. You're gonna do fine. I'll see to that."

John and Jesse rode on without talking much. They got to the pasture and started rounding up the breed cows and herding them back toward the road so they could take them back up to the ranch house. Neither man mentioned John's upcoming date until they stopped to have supper and to make camp.

"All right, Little Buddy. It's time for your first dance lesson. Come on over, we might just as well get started."

John groaned in protest. "Jesse, I don't think this is a good idea. I don't know anything about dancin' and don't think I can learn."

"It may not be a good idea," replied Jesse. "But if you don't learn from me, you're gonna take Charlotte to the dance and then she'll discover you don't know how to dance. What'll you say for yourself then?"

"You're right. I have to learn. I hope you can teach me," John added with a note of exasperation in his voice.

Jesse walked over to John and bowed sharply. "Would you care to dance?"

"What kind of question is that? We just went over that. I don't want to but I don't think I have any choice."

"You're missin' the point. That's how you ask a woman to dance. You bow and say, 'Would you care to dance?'"

"What if she says 'no'?" asked John.

"She ain't gonna say 'no.' She wants to dance with you. That's why she told you to ask her father's permission to take her to the dance. Now you try. Come over and bow and ask me if I want to dance."

John let out a long sigh, bowed to Jesse and said, "Would you care to dance?"

"Yes I would, thank you," replied Jesse.

"Now you take her by the hand like this and lead her out to the dance floor. Then you hold your left hand up like this and put your other hand high in the middle of her back. She will do the same to you. Then you just start movin' your feet and you're dancin'."

"That's all there is to it?" asked John. You just move your feet?"

"Well there's lots of different ways of moving your feet. I

don't think we have enough time to cover 'em all. The main thing is to act like you know what you are doin' and don't step on her feet. Come take my hand and let me see how you move to the music."

Jesse began humming and John started moving according to Jesse's continued instruction.

"All right, John," said Jesse. "You need to move in time with the music. Listen to me hum and try to move with the music."

John did his best but with every other step, he found himself pulling in the opposite direction as Jesse. And with every third move he was stepping on Jesse's feet.

"That's all right, Little Buddy. You're gonna get it. Just keep tryin'."

Jesse had the patience of a saint. Which is pretty remarkable, for just a month ago anyone who knew him would say he had a hair trigger and no patience at all. It seemed his bond with John had made an incredible change in the lumbering giant.

After more than two hours, Jesse was telling John he was finally getting it. And John found a new sense of confidence. He practiced bowing and then leading in a waltz, a box step, and even the basics of square dancing. The last of his lesson was to learn to dance without watching his feet.

Finally, Jesse declared him ready. "Little Buddy, you're might near as good a dancer as me. I'm right proud of you. And I'm right proud of my teachin'."

That night as John drifted off to sleep he smiled, as he anticipated taking Charlotte to the dance. Soon pleasant dreams took over. John went to sleep smiling and woke up the same way. At first light, John and Jesse started moving the cows they had rounded up. Slowly, they started them north toward the headquarters end of the ranch. The cows couldn't have been more cooperative. It was as though they knew John had a date and they needed to get up with the rest of the breed cows. John rode out front and the cows followed. Jesse lay back and urged the occasional straggler to catch up.

Shortly after noon, John and Jesse completed their journey, several hours ahead of schedule. After turning the cows into the fence, they walked over to the dining hall to see if they could rustle up something for dinner. Charlotte was there. She said she'd be glad to get them something. When she came out of the kitchen with their plates, John and Jesse thanked her and had a seat.

"You haven't forgotten about our date tonight, have you?" asked Charlotte.

"Of course not, I'll be by to pick you up after a little while."

"John, I didn't even think about it. Do you even know how

to dance?"

John and Jesse exchanged a glance and a little smile. "Of course I know how to dance. In fact, I've even gotten compliments on my dancing. I think you'll be happy."

"Well that only leaves you getting ready. I do hope you planned on taking a bath." She smiled a large grin, watching him blush.

Blushing, John said, "I just had one last week."

Jesse spoke up and said, "Don't worry, Ma'am. I'll make sure he has a bath, even if I need to scrub him myself."

"Thanks Jesse, I knew I could count on you." Then to John she added, "I'm looking forward to the dance." And with that she went back to the ranch house.

John grinned until his face hurt. Jesse laughed out loud. "Little Buddy, you've gotten yourself one whale of a woman. You better be nice to her."

"I will Jesse, you can count on it."

John wasted no time in heating water on the stove behind the bunkhouse. The only thing that stove was used for was heating water for clothes washing and an occasional bath. John stoked the stove and filled the kettle, then filled the tub about half full from the well and waited for the stove to heat the rest of his water.

Finally the water began to boil so he added it to what he

had already drawn in the bathtub. John never liked soap much but today he didn't mind it at all. After his bath, he carefully shaved and surprisingly didn't even cut himself. In the bunkhouse he grabbed a clean suit of long johns. Pulling out the only clean shirt he had, as luck would have it, it was his Sunday-go-to-meetin' shirt. He also had one clean pair of jeans and put them on. Then he looked at his boots. They were well worn. He remembered he traded a pair of custom-made boots for them in Denver to try to fit in. The boots had already been worn many a year but they replaced the last vestige of his privileged upbringing. Right now John would have given anything to have back his original pair of boots.

He rummaged around in a bin in the corner of the bunkhouse and found some bootblack and a brush. For the next hour, he worked on the old boots until they were reasonably presentable. John backed up and looked at his handy work. He was quite proud of the job he had done. The old boots were so shiny he could almost see his own reflection.

The last thing he did before he left the bunkhouse was to put on his six-gun. He thought about leaving it behind and didn't know what would be most proper. But then he thought there was a chance they might come upon a rattler and he didn't want to get caught without his gun.

John went to the barn and hitched up the buggy horse. He

spent a few minutes wiping the fenders of the buggy until he was satisfied it was as presentable as possible. It was a far cry from the buggy he had taken to school as a boy but it would do. Then he found a blanket and carefully folded it so Charlotte would be able to wrap up with it on the way home.

Out behind the barn, John found some wild flowers. He spent a few minutes picking a nice bouquet. John knew he was out of his depth, as he had never given flowers to a girl. But then again, he had never been on a date either.

As John pulled the buggy from the barn he saw that Charlotte was already waiting on the porch for him. He climbed down from the buggy and walked up the stairs to where Charlotte was sitting. He took off his hat and extended his hand giving the flowers to Charlotte.

"Hello, Ms. Charlotte. You sure look right pretty tonight."

"Thank you, Mr. Crudder. You look rather handsome yourself." John dipped his head as he felt his face flush again. He wondered if that would always happen around women or if it was just when he was around Charlotte.

"Thank you for the flowers. Let me put them in water and then we can go."

John watched her as she walked through the open door. He wasn't sure what to do with himself, so he just stood there awkwardly waiting for Charlotte to return. After a few minutes, she returned and John helped her into the buggy. He walked around to the other side, got in, and gently nudged the horse forward.

The horse had a steady, easy trot. John looked over at Charlotte a couple of times. He wanted to say something to her but words escaped him.

Charlotte finally broke the ice. "Well John, I have never seen you so handsome as you are this afternoon."

"Thank you, Ms. Charlotte."

"All right John, Ms. Charlotte was fine back at the house. But from now on, when we are by ourselves, I'm just Charlotte and you are just John."

"That's fine with me Ms . . . I mean Charlotte."

From then on John discovered Charlotte was as easy to talk to as Jesse. And she was a lot prettier. "How old are you, Charlotte?" asked John.

"I'm not sure that is a proper thing to ask, but I'm eighteen. How old are you?"

"I'm twenty-five," replied John. "Do you reckon I'm too old for you?"

"No, I think you are just the right age," said Charlotte. "Have you ever dated someone that much younger than you?"

"I'm ashamed to say I've never had a date before."

The shock showed on Charlotte's face as she turned to him

with her mouth half opened.

"You mean you have never had even one date?"

"This is the first one. I'm sorry I don't have more experience with women. I know someone with more experience would know just the right thing to say and do," offered John.

Charlotte snuggled up to John, wrapping her arms around his arm.

"You are doing just fine. And I think it is cute that you have not been on a date before. I think I am going to enjoy tonight very much."

They rode on to church talking easily about things they had in common and realized they shared many of the same values. Both had found themselves championing the cause of others who were not as privileged. They both valued education, felt it was important to acknowledge a spiritual dimension, and they loved to read.

When they arrived at the church, the dance was already underway. The sun was still about an hour from setting. John parked the buggy beside the church and gently lowered Charlotte to the ground. She relished feeling his hands on her tiny waist. And John loved the feeling of Charlotte's arms on his arms.

When she got to the ground, he kept his hands on her waist and looked deeply into her blue eyes. Charlotte smiled. John slowly leaned forward and kissed her gently on the lips. He pulled away slowly only to have Charlotte lean in and kiss him back.

John's thoughts went wild. He felt like his head was spinning. He had never felt what he felt right now. Gradually, he regained his composure and let go of Charlotte's waist. He reached down and took her hand and said, "I guess we ought to go on in."

"Yes, I guess so."

They walked in the front of the community hall that was situated right beside the church, and heard the music of a fiddle and a guitar and a cowboy singing at the top of his voice. John led her over to the side of the hall. He was getting ready to practice the first part of his lessons and ask Charlotte for a dance.

Just then she saw the marshal across the room. She waved to him and he came over to join them.

"Marshal Edwards, I would like to present Mr. John Crudder. John, this is my good friend Marshal Edwards."

John stuck out his hand. As he did he heard a loud blast followed by another. It took him a moment to realize someone had shot a gun in the building. The sound was deafening. John instinctively reached up and pushed Charlotte behind him. Then he saw the marshal collapse to the ground.

Behind him was a wild-eyed man with a smoking gun. John quickly drew his gun and fired one quick shot into the chest of the gunman.

Women screamed and the music stopped. People were running and pandemonium reigned. John confirmed that the gunman was dead and turned his attention to the marshal.

Men gathered around Marshal Edwards. John gently lifted the marshal's head. His breathing was labored and his eyes were barely open. As John watched, the marshal took one last breath and his body went limp.

John gently laid the marshal's head down. For the second time in a month, he had come face-to-face with death. And for the second time, he had used his gun to end the life of an outlaw.

As John stood up, Charlotte put her arms around him and said, "I'm so glad you were not hurt. Who was that man? Why did he shoot the marshal?"

Someone pushed through the crowd and said, "He is one of the rustlers who's been takin' everyone's cattle. He had it in for the marshal because Edwards was gettin' close to shuttin' the whole operation down. Now I wonder if they'll ever catch all of the rustlers."

John turned to Charlotte. "I better get you home. It's not proper for you to be around killin' like this."

He took her out and lifted her gently into the buggy. John quickly turned the buggy around and put the horse into a fast trot toward the H&F.

Charlotte leaned over and gave John a little peck on the cheek just as the buggy was pulling into sight of the house. She said, "John, I'm so proud of you. If it hadn't been for you, other people might have been killed."

He pulled the buggy to a stop in front of the ranch house. Slim was sitting on the porch.

"What are you doin' home so early? It's not even dark! I know I said I wanted you to have my daughter home at a decent hour, but John you could have stayed a bit longer."

"Daddy," cried Charlotte. "Someone murdered Marshal Edwards. It was awful. And if it hadn't been for John, other people would have gotten killed."

"What! What do you mean the marshal got murdered? Who would have done such a thing?"

John spoke up. "They said it was someone who was part of the rustler gang we tangled with a few weeks ago. Sir, I'm sure sorry I had your daughter at a place where she could have gotten hurt. I had no business taking her there."

"Daddy, if it hadn't been for John, there's no telling how many people would have gotten killed. John pushed me behind himself and drew his gun and killed the murderer before anyone else even knew what happened."

Slim looked at her with his jaw clinched not saying a word. Finally he turned to John and said, "I'm so glad it was you with my daughter tonight. Thank you for protectin' her. And thank you for takin' care of another of the rustlers. It seems like I am even deeper in your debt than I was before."

John said good night to both Slim and Charlotte and took the buggy to the barn. He unhitched the horse, watered it and groomed it, and went to the bunkhouse. Although he wasn't sleepy, he lay on his bunk and contemplated the events of the evening. He was asleep by the time Jesse came in, tired and ready for that cot.

The next morning, word of the marshal's murder and of John's heroics had already gotten around to the hands.

As John climbed out of his bunk, Jesse said, "Little Buddy, I heard you did it again. You killed that outlaw who gunned down the marshal and prob'ly saved a lot of lives by doin' it."

John didn't know what to say. This time he was not embarrassed by the attention. He was glad he was there to right a wrong. What surprised him was he didn't have any regrets for killing the bad man.

They went on to breakfast and the talk was all about the death of the marshal and of John's fast gun. As it turned out, several of the hands had been at the dance and had witnessed

John's lightning fast gun work. John ate his breakfast in silence. When he was through, he and Jesse got up and went to the barn where they were supposed to spend the day.

At midday, Owen came out to the barn to get John. "John, Slim wants to see you up at the house. The mayor and judge rode out and they want to have a word with you."

John had a look of concern on his face and Jesse instantly began to frown. John started toward the house and Jesse was right with him.

"Jesse, they don't want to see you," said Owen. "They only want John."

"If they've got anythin' to say to my Little Buddy, they can say it to me, too," Jesse said in a gruff voice.

John and Jesse walked quickly to the house and Owen hurried to keep up. When they got there, they found the judge, the mayor, Slim, and Charlotte gathered together talking in low voices and looking concerned.

Jesse pushed ahead, bounded up the steps of the porch and demanded, "What's this all about?"

Slim said, "Simmer down, Jesse. It's not what you think. John's not in trouble. The mayor and the judge just want to ask John something. John, this is Mayor Farley Wright. And this is Judge Gideon Anderson."

John nodded to the judge he had met a few weeks earlier,

pushed his hat back off his forehead and stuck out his hand in response to the pair doing the same. They shook hands and then the judge took control of the conversation.

"John, as you know our marshal was murdered last night. And if it hadn't been for you, other people would probably have gotten hurt. But now we find we are without a marshal. The man that murdered the marshal was part of the gang of rustlers that you took care of a few weeks ago. You got a lot of them but many more are left. They murdered the marshal because he was gettin' ready to arrest the ringleaders of the gang. And to be frank with you, we think they probably will be comin' after you next since they know how you killed many of their outlaw band."

The mayor took over. "Anyway John, we would like for you to be our new marshal. The town council met this mornin' and unanimously agreed we wanted to offer you the job. We think you're just exactly what our town needs at this crucial period. What do you say, John?"

"I don't know anything about being a marshal. I've never been a lawman before," protested John.

"Maybe not," said the judge. "But you do know the law probably better than anyone else in town since you are a lawyer. And you do know how to keep the peace. But above all John, you are the best shot and the quickest draw any of us have ever seen. I was standin' near you last night and I saw how you handled yourself. You're a natural for the job of marshal."

"Can I think about it for a while?" asked John.

The judge said, "Take all the time you need. But we need you to start work in the morning. The town can't afford to not have a marshal on duty. Word will get around quick and trouble will be brewin'."

Slim added, "John, we'll hate to lose you at the ranch. You've been a top hand. But we'll all be safer if you'll pin on the star and be our marshal, at least for a while."

Charlotte had been listening from the porch. She sidled up to John and said, "I hope you'll take the job. I would feel much better knowing that you were protecting the town."

John bowed his head in a moment of contemplation and said, "This is somethin' I've never considered. And I don't know if I will be any good at it, but if you want me, I'll take the job."

Charlotte took John's arm and held it tightly. Mayor Wright put out his hand and John shook it. Judge Anderson also shook John's hand again. Jesse patted John on the back.

Slim said, "John, you're going to make all of us real proud of you. I feel better and safer already. I know you will be a great marshal."

CHAPTER 6: 1865

John took the train from Boston to New York City. For the first time in his life he felt like his life didn't have a rudder. While he had never felt close to his parents, they had always been his guiding light. He remembered the last contact he had with his father: the telegram his father sent him after he asked if he could take money from his trust fund to help some students who were struggling financially. He appreciated his father allowing him to share his wealth. But what meant more to him than anything was his father adding: "John, I'm proud of you. I love you son." He would treasure that piece of paper for the rest of his life.

Mr. Hastings, his father's business manager, met him at the station. "Johnny, I'm so sorry about your loss. We all respected your father so much. I can't begin to imagine what you must be feeling right now."

"Thank you, Mr. Hastings. By the way, I just go by John now. Can you tell me what arrangements have been made for the funeral?"

"Certainly Sir," Hastings continued. "There is a wake tonight at the mansion and then the service will be held at Trinity Church in the morning at ten o'clock. I'm afraid your home is already running over with relatives and friends who have come by to pay their respects. You will not get much peace at the house."

"I thought that might be the case. Mr. Hastings, could you take me to the Fifth Avenue Hotel. I don't much feel like answering a lot of questions just now. Hopefully, I will feel better later and will go to the wake tonight. Could you send a carriage for me at seven this evening and then again at nine-thirty in the morning?"

"Of course, Sir." replied Hastings. "I will take care of everything for you. And may I suggest when the funeral is over the two of us go to your father's office? His attorney wants to meet with us and there are several matters that need your approval."

"That'll be fine, Mr. Hastings," John said.

Later, at the Fifth Avenue Hotel, John began to think about what he was going to do next. His father had always planned on him coming to work with him at the railroad company. In fact, his father had hinted he would be taking on a significant amount of responsibility in the company. But he had also talked about John getting some additional education specifically in business. Right now though, he didn't want to think about anything except trying to contemplate his life as a nineteen-year-old orphan.

That is the way he thought of himself—as an orphan. Sure, that was a term usually applied to young children who lost their parents. But John found himself facing an uncertain future and, for the first time in his life, he couldn't ask his father for advice.

John went to the lobby at seven and found the driver had already arrived. When the driver opened the door to the carriage, John was shocked to see Alvelda sitting there with her arms opened wide.

"Johnny, poor Johnny. Come give ol' Alvelda a hug and tell me how you're feelin'."

John fell into her arms and for the second time in as many days, John wept a river of tears. This time he sobbed bitterly as he sunk his head into Alvelda's ample bosom. She hugged him tightly and John's wailing got louder. It didn't matter. No one could hear him but Alvelda. She understood like no one else could. She had been with him through the loss of pets and dealing with schoolyard bullies. She had helped him with his studies when he was younger and was his constant companion until he left for boarding school. Alvelda was the only real anchor he felt he still had in life.

She had the carriage take an extra loop through town to give John time to compose himself. By the time they arrived at the mansion, just a few blocks from the hotel, John had wiped his eyes. Alvelda helped straighten his shirt and his suit coat. Then she took a comb from her purse and combed John's hair, just as she had done when he was a little boy.

"Now let me look at you," sighed Alvelda. "You look so handsome. You're all grown up. You are not my little Johnny Boy any more. I think it is time for you to be called John." John smiled and gently nodded his head.

Inside the mansion, relatives he had not seen in years were standing around talking, eating hors d'oeuvres, and drinking cocktails. The household staff was busy replenishing plates and filling glasses. Before John could even get into the house, several long forgotten aunts and several other relatives started hugging him and telling him how sorry they were for John. John couldn't help but wonder how many of them were sad at his parents' passing and how many were hoping to have been mentioned in Robert Crudder's will.

The formal dining room had been cleared of the massive table and all the chairs. In their place sat a funeral bier holding the open casket of Robert Crudder. As John entered the room, he could hear the well-wishers saying, "He looks so natural," and "Looks like he's just sleeping." Standing near the head of the casket was the rector of Trinity Church who spotted John as he entered the room. "Well Johnny, I am so sad for you, Laddie Boy. Your father and mother were some of the finest people God ever created. We are all going to miss them terribly."

John couldn't help but think that the priest was going to miss his father's generous contributions to the church more then they missed him. "Thank you, Father Dix."

"Johnny, I'm going to prepare a special homily for your parents. Is there anything you would like me to say at the service? Or would you perhaps like to say a few words yourself?"

"No, Father. I don't want to speak." John continued, "You just say whatever's on your heart. I know it will be just fine."

"Don't you worry about a thing. I'll see that your parents are sent off in style. And Johnny, now that you are back in New York, I hope I'll be seeing you in your old pew at Trinity come Sunday."

"I'll try Father," John said. "I don't think I'm gonna be in town long. But if I am, you can count on seein' me there."

After about thirty minutes in the house, John had enough of all the back-slapping, hugging, hysterical women crying, and half-drunk men telling him what a great man his father was and what a saint was his mother. He went outside and found his carriage waiting and gave orders to take him back to the hotel.

Arriving at the hotel, John asked the chauffeur to pick him up the next morning for the funeral. He informed him that Mr. Hastings already had that scheduled, tipped his hat and spoke to the horses as he slapped the reins. As John watched the carriage drive away, he thought of how many times he had watched his father get into a similar carriage and go off to work.

Sadness enveloped him as he went to his suite. Not long after, feeling truly alone for the first time in his life, John left his suite, went down to the restaurant, and ordered a beer. After finishing his beer, he ordered a steak and another beer. Satisfied, he returned to his suite and began to contemplate his future. He was undecided as to what he was going to do next.

Late into the evening, he finally went to bed and tried to sleep. As much as he tried, he found it difficult to rest. His mind was spinning with thoughts of his future and the absence of his parents. They didn't even get to see him graduate from Harvard. At last sleep came. As he drifted off, he thought again of his father's last words to him. *John, I'm proud of you. I love you son.*

John slept late the next morning, dressed for the funeral, and then went down for breakfast. He picked up a copy of the

New York Times at the front desk and then had a seat in the restaurant. The banner headline read, *CRUDDER DEAD!*

John read a bit of the story.

Robert Crudder, railroad magnate, financier, and leading New York City businessman, was killed along with his wife, Lucille, in a buggy accident two days ago, less than two blocks from his Fifth Avenue mansion. Crudder and his wife were leaving for a breakfast meeting with friends when their horse was startled by a passing fire engine, upending the buggy and ending the couple's lives.

Known best for building the Great National Railroad, Crudder and his wife were strong financial supporters of New York Philharmonic-Symphony Orchestra. They were also active members at Trinity Church, where their funerals will take place at ten o'clock this morning with The Reverend Morgan Dix officiating.

John couldn't read any more. He tried to eat breakfast but found he had no appetite. He went back to the newspaper but found most of the stories were about his father's empire and the impact he had made not only on New York City, but also on the nation. Yes, John was proud of his father but he was also more focused on his own grieving.

The stately Trinity Church was visible over much of the city. It was the tallest building in New York. At two hundred eighty-one feet, Trinity Church was also the tallest building in the entire United States. John recalled learning the current building was the third to be built on that site. He remembered his parents telling him he was the first baby to be christened there when the building was completed in 1846.

When the carriage arrived at the church, John climbed down and walked through the doors. He went down to the second pew from the front to the left of the altar—the same pew he had sat on throughout his growing up years. He listened to the rector make a few comments about his mother, but it seemed like most of his remarks were about his father. John got the feeling the priest was trying to talk God into letting his father into heaven. But from what John knew of his parents, he knew his father and mother were already enjoying their final reward.

After the service, John stood and walked with the rector as they preceded the casket down the center aisle to the cemetery next door. He thought it fitting his father would be buried just a few feet away from many other famous people including Alexander Hamilton, William Bradford, Robert Fulton, many heroes of the American Revolution, and others.

While John tried to listen to the graveside service, he realized his thoughts were elsewhere. Following the service, Mr. Hastings approached John. "I think that was a fine tribute to your parents. The world will not be as bright of a place without them."

"I agree with you, Mr. Hastings. I wonder if you would tell Father Dix I would like to speak with him and I would like you to be there as well.

Mr. Hastings made arrangements and shortly after the service, the three of them sat down in the rector's office.

"Thank you, Father Dix, for your words. I know my parents would have been pleased. In the next few days, Mr. Hastings will be contacting you to let you know of the bequest my father has left for the church. I do not know what it will be but I want you to know that whatever he has left, I will match in my will."

"That is very generous of you, John. I know we will want to have a nice memorial erected to your parents that is in keeping with their generous gift."

"Actually, that is what I wanted to talk to you about. I too want them to be remembered and for their name to live on. However, I have something much more simple in mind. While I was sitting on the pew where I have sat with my parents for so many years, I thought it would be fitting to have a little brass plaque there on the pew."

"Well certainly we can do that," replied the rector in surprise. "However, I thought there should be something much more elaborate to recognize their contribution to the community and especially to Trinity Church."

"It would please me if you would just place a simple plaque in their memory," John replied. "If you will get me a pen and paper, I will write out what I want to be engraved on the plaque."

The pastor got paper and a pen and stood from his desk inviting John to take a seat. John bowed his head to contemplate and after a few minutes wrote:

1865

To be forever free

this pew is given to

TRINITY CHURCH

in memory of

Robert and Lucille Crudder

by their son

John Crudder

"John, I'm glad to do that," lamented the surprised minister, "but I know that your father left us much more than the value of the pew."

"I know you are right, but I think this would be most fitting. Their names will be remembered in the church, but they are not celebrated for their wealth or their gifts to the church."

"John, as I think about it, I'm sure your father would agree with you. I see a lot of his greatness in you."

With that, John and Mr. Hastings left the pastor's office. As they walked toward the front of the church, John said, "Yesterday, you said we needed to meet with my father's lawyer. I'm ready if you are."

"I am, John. We can take my carriage. Then when we're through, you can take my carriage back to your hotel."

They rode to Robert Crudder's office and found that his attorney was already waiting for them. After introductions, John and Mr. Hastings took a seat and listened as the attorney read through the will.

The attorney said, "John, this is all pretty standard. But there is one part that I want to read to you."

Beyond the bequests I'm leaving to the New York Philharmonic-Symphony Orchestra and Trinity Church, I leave all my earthly possessions, including my company, all stocks and investments, to my only son Jonathan William Crudder. If he is less than twenty-one years of age, the company will be held in trust and continue to be run by my longtime business manager Howard Hastings.

The following is for John.

John, I prepared this will when you went off to boarding school at Georgetown. Since my plan was to update it after we had worked side-by-side for several years, it is obvious that I did not live to get that opportunity and you are now responsible for my company. I know I am leaving it in good hands. I don't know where you are in your schooling. If you are not yet twenty-one, I hope you will continue your education at Harvard. When you graduate, I would suggest that you broaden your horizons by studying business at a university in Europe. Mr. Hastings will know my most current thoughts about where I would suggest you continue your studies.

I know you will make me proud, John. I may never have told you that I'm proud of you and that I love you. I have tried so many times before but somehow just couldn't come up with the right words. But John, I am proud of you and I do love you with all my heart. Know that you will always have my approval for whatever decisions you make in life.

John was stunned by what he heard. Tears came to his eyes as he heard his father once again speak of his love and pride in him. Why couldn't he ever say that to his face?

John contemplated his father's words. Then he focused on the fact his father had left his company completely to him. He knew he would be well taken care of by his father but he never dreamed he would leave his entire company to him. John didn't know a thing about running a company of any size, much less one of the leading companies in America.

He turned to Mr. Hastings and said, "What am I supposed to do? I don't know anything about business. I would wreck the company! What was he thinking to leave his company to me?"

Mr. Hastings dismissed the attorney and sat down with John. "Your father knew this would come as a shock to you. He also believes you will do him proud."

"He talked about studying business in Europe. Do you know what he was talking about?"

"Just last week he told me that he hoped you would go to the University of Oxford in England. He believed they have the best educational opportunity for you after your work at Harvard. He also said that would help you understand why in your language studies he was never content with you learning only Latin. He always insisted you study ancient Greek. You fought against it for a while, but then you embraced it and seemed to love it. Both of those languages are required for acceptance into Oxford."

"So he's been planning on this for a long time? Why didn't he ever tell me about it? I knew he wanted me to go to Harvard but he never mentioned me studying business in Europe. When was he planning on telling me?"

"As soon as you finished Harvard, he was going to tell you. And he wasn't going to make the decision for you. He wanted to see if you were motivated enough to get the business education you needed."

"Once again, I find myself speechless. For many years, I have felt he was making all my decisions for me. I expected to feel pressured into going to Europe to study but I don't. That actually makes good sense. I got a wonderful education at Harvard but I am not ready to take over his company. So, Mr. Hastings, if you don't mind, would you have someone make arrangements for me to go to England? It seems I have a new motivation for continuing my education."

Mr. Hastings nodded his approval. John rose, shook Mr. Hastings' hand, and returned to his hotel to begin the next chapter of his life

CHAPTER 7: 1871

John was sworn in as marshal in a small ceremony in Judge Anderson's chambers at the courthouse. Mayor Wright was there, as was Harvey Fowler, the owner of the bank. Also in attendance were Sally Jenson, who owned the Better Days Hotel, and Betsy Hawkins, who owned the Cheer Up Saloon and Seth Davis the owner of the Davis Mercantile. They all congratulated John and said how grateful they were to him for taking the job as marshal.

Looking down at the badge on his chest, John wondered if he was making the right decision. He thought it a bit ironic that he came to Bandera to be a champion of the law. Little did he realize that meant wearing a badge and a gun instead of carrying law volumes and wearing a suit.

After checking out the marshal's office and confirming the

jail was empty, John took his first stroll through downtown as marshal. Everywhere he went people greeted him by name. Some called him John. Others called him Marshal; then when he got to the Cheer Up Saloon, he found the patrons were already schooled on how to address him. "Hello, Marshal Crudder," several called to him.

The rest of the day, John went from business to business introducing himself and getting acquainted with the owners. He then went back to the marshal's office to see if he could find his deputy. When he got there, he found the deputy asleep with his feet on the desk.

John closed the door a bit louder than necessary, but it woke up the deputy. The sleepy man looked up and said, "How can I help you? Oh, I see you're a lawman, too. Where ya from, Marshal?"

"My name is John Crudder. Are you Clem?"

"I am. And I was asking you, Marshal, where ya from?" asked the deputy.

"Well I'm actually from New York City. But if you wonder where I work, I work here. I'm the new marshal. Glad to meet you, Clem."

John stuck out his hand as the startled deputy struggled to his feet and stuck out his hand. "I thought I was going to be the next marshal," said the deputy.

"Well I'm sorry you got the word like this," John replied. "I just found out myself. I was out working on the H&F when the judge and mayor asked if I'd be the next marshal."

Recognition came to the slow-witted deputy. "You're the one! You're the one who shot the marshal's killer. And you killed the rest of them rustlers on the H&F. Right?"

"I reckon that's me. But neither of those things was that big of a deal. I was just doing what anyone else would have done in the same place."

"Well Marshal. I don't rightly know what to say. I was countin' on the job. But now I guess you are even gonna get a new deputy."

"Actually, Clem. I'd be obliged if you would continue as my deputy. I know I will never fill Marshal Edward's boots and I've got lots to learn about bein' a lawman. I was hopin' you'd help me and show me the ropes."

Clem stood up straight, put his shoulders back, and smiled. He stuck out his hand and said, "I'd be pleased to help you all I can, Marshal. There's a lot to know about this town and this job. I'm the man you need. You can count on me."

John went down to the Better Days Hotel and found Sally Jenson had been anticipating him stopping by. "Well Marshal," Sally said, "I was wondering when you would come by. Are you ready to see your room?"

The surprise on John's face let Sally know he had no idea what she was talking about. "The town provides a room for the marshal in my hotel. Anyway if you want to stay here, I would be pleased to have you. And the bill for your room and your meals goes to the city. That is just part of your salary."

"I'd be pleased to stay here Ma'am," said John. "I was just coming to see about rentin' a room. I had no idea this'd be part of my pay."

"We figure it's to our advantage to provide you a room. That way we know you'll be in town most days. I guess it's a bit selfish of us but we've found it's an arrangement that benefits both you and the town."

John thought he was going to find the job to his liking. And for several days, he couldn't have asked for anything more. The town folks were great. There was not much crime; in fact the only thing he had to do for the first few weeks was to break up a couple of fights at the Cheer Up Saloon.

One day Charlotte came to town in a buggy to do some shopping at Davis Mercantile. John was walking down the boardwalk when Charlotte brought her buggy to a stop. He walked over to her, took off his hat, and said, "Howdy, Ms. Charlotte. I'm pleased to see you."

"And it's good to see you too, Marshal," she said as she stood to get out of the buggy. John replaced his hat and put his hands on Charlotte's waist and gently lifted her to the ground. He remembered very well the sweet kiss he got the first time he did that. But this time he backed up, tipped his hat, and turned to go.

"By the way, Marshal. My father told me if I ran into you, he would take it as a favor if you would come to supper tonight. We're eating in the house. It will just be family."

"I would be pleased to, Ms. Charlotte. Tell your father I'll be there a little before dark." And with that John walked back toward the marshal's office. He felt like he hardly had his feet on the ground. Smiling to himself, John realized he had missed seeing Charlotte. He never knew he could feel that way about a woman.

The afternoon passed slowly as John anticipated seeing Charlotte again. Finally, he cleaned up, changed his shirt, and set off for the H&F. Midnight went into a fast lope just as soon as he headed south toward the ranch. He seemed to know exactly where they were headed.

When he arrived at the H&F, John was greeted by 'hellos' and 'howdys' from several of the hands. Then he heard, "Hey Little Buddy, is that really you?"

John dismounted and went over to Jesse. He stuck out his hand but Jesse just grabbed him up and hugged him like he was a rag doll. John laughed and said, "Jesse, you're going to squeeze all the stuffin' out of me."

"You gonna have supper with us?" asked Jesse.

"No, Slim wanted to see me. I'm going to eat in the house with him," replied John.

"I don't reckon Charlotte will be there, will she?"

John blushed. "You know Jesse, I don't know who'll be there." He gave Jesse a little smile and walked over to the house. Charlotte came out of the door and greeted him. "Hello again Ms. Charlotte. Is your father here?"

"He sure is, Marshal," said Charlotte. "He's inside; come on in."

John entered the house and took off his hat. Slim came into the room and said, "Well hello, Marshal. I'm so glad you could join us for supper."

"I was pleased to get the invitation, Mr. Hanson."

"Now Marshal, remember it's just Slim."

"All right, Slim. And please just call me John like always. I still haven't gotten used to everyone calling me Marshal."

As they sat down to supper Slim said, "That's fine John. How's the new job coming? Any problems?"

"To tell you the truth, I feel like I'm not earning my keep. I just walk around town talkin' to people. In two weeks on the job, the only thing I have ever done is break up two fights at the saloon. And there wasn't much to either of them. Oh, and I did discover Mr. Davis left the door to the mercantile open one night. I make rounds a couple of times a night but even that seems like it's not needed. Bandera is a quiet and peaceful town. The liveliest place in town is the saloon and most of the customers are locals except on the weekends when hands from the outlying ranches come to town. But even then, there is just a little drinkin' and playin' poker. There's very little trouble there. Are you sure this town even needs a marshal?"

"Things may be quiet here now but it is not always like that," said Slim. "Remember how you came to get the job. There was a murder right in the middle of town. And there has been a lot of rustlin' around here for years. That's not all. Several of the smaller ranchers are getting pressured to sell out. There is more going on in this town than is apparent."

"That's the first I've heard about people being pressured to sell out," said John. "When did that start?"

"It's been going on for years. The heck of it is that we can't figure out who is pressurin' 'em. There is always a different situation. One rancher complained that his well got poisoned. Another said someone was killin' off his calves and makin' it look like coyotes were responsible. Another had taken out several loans to cover losses through the years. He finally decided he would never be able to repay them so he sold out. It's never the same circumstance. It just seems like there's somethin' goin' on beneath the surface. We've even had more problems on the H&F than I've told others about."

"What are you talking about, Daddy?" asked Charlotte. "I've never heard anything about problems here."

Slim said, "Well the rustlers you and Jesse discovered had been stealin' from us for years. And there have been times when our wells just didn't seem to be producin' enough water. And a couple of years ago, right after we cut our hay and stacked it into the barn, the barn burned down. The fire captain said it was 'spontaneous combustion' brought about by putting up green hay when it was still wet. But here's the thing, John. That hay was not green or wet. I have been puttin' up hay all my life. I know how to do it the right way."

John made a frown and thought for a moment. "Slim, I had no idea those things were goin' on. Do you have any idea who's behind it?"

"I've never said this to anyone but I'm afraid it is one of the town leaders. There are times I have suspected each one of them. I've even had suspicions about Sally Jenson and Betsy Hawkins. But then there wouldn't be anything to go with any of those suspicions. I would watch closely and wait for something else to happen that would implicate one of them but I couldn't ever put it together."

"That just doesn't make sense," said John. "I can't see any

of them being involved in the things you have talked about. They seem as honest as can be. In fact, I have been impressed with each of them."

"I'm not surprised to hear that, John. For a long time, I've had the same thoughts," replied Slim. "But there has to be someone behind these things. It's not as though we're a big city like Austin or San Anton. It wouldn't be surprisin' to see those things there. But not here in Bandera."

John listened and nodded. He didn't know what to make of what Slim was saying. If it had been anyone else telling him these things, John would have questioned that person's grip on reality. But he knew Slim to be rational and level-headed.

"John, there's somethin' else you should know," Slim said. "Just before Marshal Edwards was murdered, he told me he found out about a big conspiracy in town. He didn't name names but he did tell me he was going to send for the Texas Rangers to come and investigate. I'm thinkin' he must have told the same thing to someone else. He was murdered two days later. I asked the telegraph operator if Marshal Edwards had sent any telegrams in the previous week and he said he hadn't."

This all came as a surprise to John. He had thought this was the quietest and most peaceful town he had ever known. How could such crime be taking place right under everyone's noses?

"Slim, who else have you told about this?" asked John.

"No one but Marshal Edward and you—yeah now you, Charlotte."

"Here's what I think," John expressed. "Don't either of you breathe a word of this to anyone. Give me some time to do some investigatin'. If there's somethin' goin' on there, I'll find out what it is."

"I think you will at that, John," said Slim. "You do your investigatin'. Just don't let anyone else know what you're doin' 'cause I think then your life might be in danger."

Charlotte's eyes got big and she put her hand to her mouth.

"Don't either of you worry about me. I'll be careful. And you can be sure I'll get to the bottom of this. It may take some time but I'll figure it out.

"Thanks John," said Slim. "I know you will."

With that, John got up from the table and said, "Thanks kindly for supper, I really enjoyed it. And thanks for cluin' me on somethin' I knew nothin' about."

Charlotte walked John out to the porch. "Would you like to sit on the porch for a while? I just made a pitcher of lemonade."

John hesitated, knowing he wanted to but feeling unsettled about what he had heard from Slim. "Charlotte, I would love to. I hope you know that, but after what your father told me, I think I need to get back to town and see what's really goin' on."

Charlotte looked sad. "I was afraid you'd say that. I hope

you'll come out again soon. I don't like going so long between visits with you. I like you and I… Well I want to spend time with you. So, whenever you can, please find time to come and see me."

"I will, Charlotte. You can count on it," said John. "I like you too. If it were up to me, I would stay a while longer tonight. But I feel like I have to put the business of Bandera first—at least for now."

John mounted Midnight and headed back to town. He had a bad feeling about what he was going to find with his investigation. And he didn't know what he would do if what he suspected was true.

CHAPTER 8: 1866

Mr. Hastings telegraphed Harvard and asked them to send John's transcript to the University of Oxford. The English school wired back immediately they would be pleased to accept John Crudder into their school to study business. He then booked passage for John on the RMS Scotia.

John boarded the steamship for his nine-day voyage to Queenstown, Ireland. The ship offered only first-class accommodations. The four-hundred-foot ship spellbound John. As the steam whistle signaled their departure, stewards filled champagne glasses. During the voyage, John spent his time reading and studying. He had brought with him a variety of business books. He was determined to become the best businessman possible. John wanted nothing more than for his father's pride in him to be justified.

Arriving in Queenstown, John traveled to Oxford, England, by carriage and boat. Immediately upon arrival, John gave himself completely to his studies. He found the course work challenging but not beyond what he could handle. In fact, he found he had the capacity to take on a larger class load than was recommended. After successfully petitioning the administration, he enrolled in several additional classes.

Unlike his time at Harvard, John felt he needed to cram as much education into as little time as possible. He would turn twenty-one in less than two years and was determined to graduate and be back in New York before that birthday. That was the time he would take over his father's company.

As part of his studies, John took a couple of courses in business law and found he had an affinity for law courses. He even wondered if things had been different and he was free to choose his own course of study if he might decide to be a lawyer. But he pushed those thoughts out of his mind. In less than two years he would be back in New York as a railroad executive.

* * * * * *

Those two years passed quicker than John could have imagined. Back in New York, John started working in his father's old office. Mr. Hastings was a patient tutor, teaching him all about the railroad industry. It was obvious to John why his father depended so much on Mr. Hastings.

As with everything John tackled, he became absorbed with running his company. He learned all there was to know about railroads. He kept Mr. Hastings close and used him as a constant advisor and thinking partner.

John was appalled with some of the unethical behavior he observed in others. He found numerous businessmen and politicians who were dishonest but were able to hide their illegal behavior behind shell companies and middlemen. As he gained expertise at understanding his own company, he was happy he could find no evidence that his father had ever cheated anyone.

The more John looked at the shady dealings of others, the more he wished he could do something to right the wrongs he saw. He knew only the sharpest of attorneys would be able to build a case against these scoundrels. But he also knew as long as these crooked businessmen had the cooperation of dishonest politicians, nothing would change.

In a moment of honesty, John admitted to himself that he was bored with his work. His passion was in seeing justice served. He thought back to how he had loved the study of business law at Oxford. The next several weeks were used contemplating how he was going to spend the rest of his life. After a couple of months, John had a talk with Mr. Hastings and let him know his innermost feelings.

"Mr. Hastings, my heart is just not in this work. Maybe if my father had lived, I would have enjoyed working with him. But I'm even afraid I would still have grown bored with business."

Hastings was silent for a couple of minutes. Finally, he said, "John, I have seen for some time you were not happy. I had hoped things would change as you got more involved in the business. I also know you well enough to know that you have already given some thought to your future. What are you thinking about?"

"Believe it or not, I think I'll go back to school. I want to study law and become an attorney. Harvard has a top law school. I think I will start there with the new school year in a few weeks. I have already communicated with them and have been accepted."

"What about the company?" asked Hastings.

"I'm going to sell it all," said John. "There is no use keeping it. I'll never want to come back to it."

Hastings was stunned. He couldn't imagine the company ever being owned by someone outside the Crudder family. John had anticipated his shock.

"Mr. Hastings," John added, "when I sell it, it will be with one proviso. That is that you be the chief executive officer for your lifetime. And with it will come a salary that is in keeping with your new responsibility. You have run the company by yourself for the past four years anyway. And even over this past year as we worked together, you took a lot of effort letting me think I was making the decisions, but we both know that I never made a decision without you.

"Oh yes, the mansion on Fifth Avenue is yours, too. However, I want you to promise you will keep on all of the household staff. They have been there for years. And I consider them all family. Especially Alvelda."

Hastings' eyes grew bigger. His mouth opened and closed a couple of times without any sound coming out. Then he said, "I don't know what to say."

"Just say yes," said John. "And your first order of business is to sell the company. Make the best deal you can. The better the deal you make, the better it will be for you. And as a reward for the lifetime of service you provided to my father, you will receive two percent of the selling price. That should be enough to allow you to live handsomely for the rest of your life."

Hastings dropped his head and placed his elbows on his knees. After a couple of minutes, he smiled and said, "Mr. John

Crudder, it would be my pleasure to accept your generous offer. I will be the best CEO any company ever had. And I want to add that I think your father would be proud of the man you've become and of the decision you've made today."

* * * * * *

Back at Harvard, John felt like he was home. The four years he spent at the university previously had been the best of his life so far. He found the study of law enlightening. Unlike his previous studies, he felt that study was teaching him to think critically rather than just memorizing facts and figures. Of course, there were plenty of things he needed to learn and remember, but for the most part he felt that the study of law was truer to what he felt education should be.

John reverted to the study plan he had when he first came to Harvard. He was determined to stay a full three years studying the law. He was in no hurry to leave the school and had no desire to rush his legal education.

One of the greatest gifts of his time at law school was his deepening desire to see wrongs righted—to see injustice come to an end. John felt like he had the Scales of Justice in his head. When he saw the scales out of balance, he could not rest until he saw that balance restored.

Finally, John completed his degree and received his diploma. He was convinced Mr. Hastings was right: his father would have been proud of his decision to chart his own course. John wanted nothing more than to spend his life pursuing justice.

His plan was to head west, find a place that needed a lawyer, and open a law office. He felt the perfect situation would be to find a small town that had never had a lawyer and to work there. John wanted to see as much of the country as possible but his ultimate goal was to find a place in Texas he could call home.

CHAPTER 9: 1871

Back in Bandera, John Crudder tried to figure out what was really going on in the town. His suspicion immediately went to the town council. On the surface, that didn't make any sense. They all appeared to be upstanding business people. There was nothing about their dealings with him that caused him to doubt they were anything other than what they presented. But he also knew they seemed to all be more successful than what could be accounted for by honest business practices. And they all had land holdings that increased as various small ranchers sold out and left town.

John thought if he were right he would need proof that

didn't seem to exist. He also knew just as it was with the crooked businessmen in New York, if they did have any politicians on the payroll, they were protected and could continue to operate with impunity. John had no evidence Judge Gideon Anderson and Mayor Farley Wright were anything other than honest. But he also realized that if they were part of a conspiracy with the rest of the council, they would be virtually unstoppable.

As he came downstairs for breakfast, he spotted the hotel owner Sally Jenson.

"Ms. Jennings, would you join me for breakfast?"

"Hello, Marshal. I'd be glad to." John stood and pulled her chair out for her. "So, I hope your accommodations are to your liking."

"They certainly are, Ms. Jennings."

"I think it's time for you to call me Sally."

"I'll do that if you can just call me John."

"John, I'll do that. But when there are others around, I think I need to address you as Marshal."

"That makes sense," said John. "So tell me about yourself. How did you get into the hotel business?"

"Well, my husband died about ten years ago. He was a rancher and I knew I couldn't keep the ranch going by myself. So, I sold my ranch to the judge. Gideon turned out to be quite a friend. I don't know what I would have done without him. He's the one who convinced me to open a hotel. He said the town was large enough to need one and no one had yet tried. He arranged for Harvey over at the bank to loan me the additional money I needed. And he even arranged for me to not have to make payments on the loan until the hotel was profitable."

"How long did that take?" asked John.

"I was in the black within six months," replied Sally. "And I actually was able to pay off the loan in just a couple of years. Things have been good ever since. How about you, John? Tell me more about yourself."

"Well, there's not much to tell," said John. "I grew up in New York City. My dad was a businessman and he wanted me to join him in business but I preferred to go to law school instead. I just couldn't see myself living in the big city wearing a suit every day. So, I came out west looking for a place to open a law office. I liked the look of Bandera and thought this would be a great place to live. That was just a few months ago. I love the law but realized there wasn't much need for a lawyer around here. For the little bit of legal work that's needed, people just ride into San Anton."

John surprised himself at the many things he left out of his history. He made no mention of his father's amazing success as a railroad tycoon. And he didn't even mention his parents' death.

"So John, I have to tell you that I wish I were ten years younger. You're a handsome man. I would be givin' Charlotte a run for her money."

At first, John blushed at the compliment but then he was alarmed. "What do you mean about Charlotte?"

"John, you can't keep a secret in this town. Everyone knows you're sweet on her. You were at the dance with her when Marshall Edwards died."

John found it interesting that she made no reference to the fact that cause of death was murder. Was he making too much of her words? Maybe she was just so proper she didn't think it seemly to use the word murder. Surely, that was it.

"Well thanks for the compliment. But I'm not sweet on anyone." John tried to sell the lie. He could tell by the smile on Sally's face that he was not successful.

"Whatever you say, John. I think Charlotte's a lovely woman. And I should add, a lucky woman."

"Sally, do you miss life on the ranch?"

"I did at first," replied Sally. "But I've grown

accustomed to living in town. I've actually bought a couple of small ranches over the years and thought a time or two about moving out to one of them. But I realize I belong in town so I have a foreman on each one running things for me. I've found I have a good head for business. I run the ranches just like I run my hotel. And each of them is very profitable."

"Well congratulations, Sally. You must be proud of yourself. You have become quite the businesswoman."

"Thank you, kind sir. I have certainly enjoyed visiting with you. Duty calls. I need to see to some of my other guests."

"I have enjoyed our visit as well, Sally. Maybe we can do it again sometime."

Her eyes flashed and she smiled as she turned to leave.

John headed back to the marshal's office. Clem was there drinking coffee. "Hello, Marshal," said Clem as he jumped to his feet and started shuffling papers. "I was jus' goin' through the new wanted posters and tryin' to straighten up a bit."

"That's fine, Clem," said John. "Have a seat. You don't have to jump up every time I walk in."

"All right, Marshal. Oh, and Ms. Sally sent over

breakfast for the prisoner. How much longer are we going to keep him?"

"Drunk and disorderly is three days. I guess we'll let him out in the morning. When you get a chance, go see Ms. Hawkins at the saloon and see how much it will cost to replace what he broke."

"Shor 'nuff, Marshal."

"And Clem," added John, "I meant to tell you that you did a good job arresting him. I heard from Ms. Hawkins that you broke up the fight and restored order quickly."

"Why thanks, Marshal."

"Clem, how long have you lived in Bandera?"

"I was born here. Lived here my whole entire life."

"How long has Judge Anderson been in town?" asked the marshal.

"He's been here forever. My pappy said he was made judge back in '44. The reason I remember is that's the same year I was born."

"Seems like he's well liked," said John.

"Yup. Most everyone likes him," said Slim, "'Cepting those who have to face him in court."

"What do people say about the judge?" asked John.

"Mostly they say he's a fair judge. And they say he is

generous, helping out when someone is down on their luck. Just last year, he helped the Widder Jones. After her husband got killed, he helped her make payments on her ranch, 'til she just didn't want to continue. Then the judge himself bought the ranch so she'd have nuff money to move to San Anton to be with her sister."

"Did you get to talk to Ms. Jones before she left town?" asked John.

"You know," Clem said, "that's the thing. One day she was here in town. I saw her down at the mercantile. She didn't say nothin' ah'tall about leavin'. But the next day she sold out to the judge and left town."

"Has anything like that happened before?"

"Which part? The judge helping people out or people leavin' town sudden like?"

"Both."

"Well now that I think about it there's been a right smart number of people who leave town without tellin' anybody. I guess I've kind of gotten used to it. Don't seem so out of place no more."

"And what about the judge helpin' other people?" the marshal asked.

"Yup, he's always helpin' someone. I 'member when I

was a little boy, we didn't have a bank. My pappy said the judge loaned Harvey Fowler money enough to get it started."

"How would a judge have enough money to open a bank?" asked John.

"Don't know. But he seems to have all he needs and is always willing to help others in need. I know he either loaned money himself or had Mr. Fowler loan it to 'bout every business in town. He's always helpin' someone. He even helped me once."

"When was that, Clem?"

"Well, it was after my pappy died. I was only nineteen then. I never was much of a hand at ranching. I put our old home place up for sale. Didn't seem like nobody would buy it. I didn't know what I was gonna do. Someone told me I ought to tell the judge and see if he would help me. So, that's what I did. He asked me if he was able to arrange for someone to buy it if I would be willing to take less for it. I didn't know much about what land was worth. But the next day Ms. Sally said she'd buy it if I wanted to sell."

"So you cut the price?" asked John.

"Yup," said Clem. "I only got half as much as I was askin'. But it was more money than I'd ever seen. I spent a lot of it pretty quick. I didn't know how fast money could get away. I lost most of it playin' poker over at the Cheer Up."

"I didn't know you played poker," said John.

"Well I never did before or since. But that night I got drunk and I started playin' poker. I was real lucky, at least at first. I had a pile of money on the table. I got good at knowin' how to bet and how to raise. Before I knowed it I was bettin' hundreds of dollars on each hand. Then I started losin'. Before I knowed it, I lost everythin'."

"Who'd you lose it to?" asked John.

"Well see, that's the thing. I never saw 'em before, just a couple of strangers. They were gone by the next mornin'. I complained to the judge but he said there was nothin' he could do since I was the one who decided to play poker."

"Did that make you mad?" asked John.

"Not really. He was right. It was my own fault. But you know what he did? He took me over to see Marshal Edwards and got him to give me the job of deputy. That was nine years ago. I don't know what I'd've done without the judge."

"It sounds like the judge is a pretty popular man," said John.

"You've got that right. He's a really good man."

"Well Clem, I'm gonna make my rounds now. You hang around the jail since we've got a prisoner. I'll be back by noon and relieve you."

"All right, Marshal."

John walked over to the livery stable and checked on Midnight. He wanted to get him out for a ride. Maybe he'd ride out to the H&F and see how Charlotte was doing.

He walked on through town until he got to the judge's house. He'd never been inside but thought since the judge has a sign showing where his office is, he must be fine with having folks drop by.

He walked up to the door and read a sign that read, *wipe your feet and come on in.* John walked in and removed his hat. A little bell rang as he closed the door. There was a large parlor that was filled with beautiful furniture. A massive chandelier hung from the center of the room.

The judge's housekeeper came into the parlor and said, "May I help you?"

"I was wonderin' if the judge is in. I'm Marshal Crudder."

"Hello Marshal, I'm Cora Potter. I'm the judge's housekeeper and cook."

"Pleased to meet you Ma'am."

"Just have a seat, Marshal. I'll tell the judge you're here."

John settled into a couch that was every bit as fine as anything he had known growing up. It was obvious that the judge had significant financial resources. After about five minutes, the judge walked in.

"Well Marshal, to what do I owe the pleasure?"

"I was just out makin' my rounds and thought I would stop by to see your office. I must say, I'm impressed. I've not seen such a fine office since I left New York."

"It's nice but it's really not that much," said the judge. "I just like to have a comfortable place to work."

"It certainly is comfortable, Judge."

"Marshal, I'm glad you stopped by. I was going to come see you later this week. A couple of us have been thinking. We know of a ranch that is going to go up for sale in a couple of weeks. We were thinking it might be a good investment for you."

"I can't afford to buy a ranch." John didn't let on that he was wealthy beyond anything the judge could imagine.

"Actually, we have it all worked out. Harvey will loan you the money for the ranch. It is priced right so you would be getting quite a bargain. And there's cattle on the ranch;

you should be able to sell off about half the herd to clear the loan. It's not a big ranch. Only about one section. But it would be a good way to get started in ranching. Kind of something to look forward to in retirement."

"I don't really know what to say. That's mighty generous of you, but for right now, I just want to concentrate on being marshal and not be thinkin' about becomin' a land owner. By the way, who is the 'we' you were talking about?"

"The town council. We had a meeting last night and someone had heard the ranch was going to be for sale. We thought it would be a nice way to make you feel welcomed and help you plant some deep roots in Bandera."

"I'm much obliged to you and the council. And thanks for understandin' that I want to just concentrate on my job for now."

"That's quite all right, Marshal. Actually, it was Sally that was going to give up her turn for you."

"What do you mean—give up her turn?" asked John.

"Well, being on the council, we learn about opportunities from time to time. We just take turns so that everyone gets a chance at a good deal," said the judge.

"You mean everyone on the council, that is."

"Sure. Each member of the council gets to share in those opportunities. It is just one of the little perks that comes with our service to the community. After all, we serve the town for nothing. Not a single one of us takes a salary for being on the council. We do it out of the goodness of our hearts."

"That's mighty nice, Judge. I 'preciate y'all makin' me feel so at home. I really like it here in Bandera."

"And we're glad you're here," replied the judge.

"Well Judge, I better get on about my rounds. It was nice visitin' with you. And thanks again for all you've done to make me feel welcomed.

John left the judge's office and resumed his rounds. As he walked from business to business, he thought about the judge's offer. It was as if he were offering to give him the ranch. He would go through the formality of getting a loan, only to turn around and sell enough cattle to wipe away the mortgage. Why would they be so generous to him? It didn't make sense unless they were hoping to make him so indebted that they could control him.

Back at the office, he found Clem where he had left him. Only this time he was taking a nap. As John closed the door, Clem awakened and jumped to his feet. "Howdy,

Marshal. I must have dozed off for a second."

"That's all right, Clem. Hey, I was thinkin' about Marshal Edwards. Did he own any land?"

"Funny you should ask. He didn't used to own none ah'tall. Then about five years ago, he started buyin' small ranches. I think he had ten or twelve of them by the time he died. He always said they was goin' to be for his retirement someday. A shame he never got 'round to being able to enjoy 'em."

"I wonder what happened to his land," asked John.

"You know, that's another funny thing. The judge said he left a will that deeded the ranches to various members of the town council. I guess he felt grateful for the way they had helped him through the years."

"What do you mean, helped him?" asked John.

"Well, they were the ones who told him when there was a good deal to be made on a ranch. And Mr. Fowler even loaned him the money. But they were all such good deals that he always paid off each loan pretty quickly."

CHAPTER 10: 1870

John Crudder fell in love with horses when he was in prep school. Flame had been his first and only horse. He was a small horse that fit his small frame; the perfect horse for a boy. But with his impending trip west, he knew it was time for him to have a horse more suited to a man.

While still undecided about the horse he would buy, he knew he wanted a stallion that was tall and fast. Beyond that, he was open. Oh yes, and he didn't want another chestnut or any brown color

John read about an auction for thoroughbred horses at the Union Course racetrack. He studied up on thoroughbreds and found they had been popular in Europe for a long time and had been in America for more than one hundred and fifty years. John went to the auction to see if he would find a horse that suited him. The third horse on the block was a magnificent black stallion with a white blaze star on his face and four tall white socks.

The first horse went for fifteen hundred dollars. It was a beautiful bay that stood seventeen hands. Second on the block was a chestnut that stood sixteen and a half hands and fetched twelve hundred dollars.

"The next horse has a great pedigree that goes back to England. But as you can see, he's only fifteen hands tall and," the auctioneer paused and smiled, "as you can plainly see, he has four white socks." John knew horse people had a number of superstitions and had heard that a horse with white socks was thought to have softer hoofs and was not as desirable.

The gathered buyers laughed and chanted with the auctioneer as they recited a poem in unison:

One white sock, keep him to the end,
Two white socks, give him to a friend,
Three white socks, send him far away,
Four white socks, keep him not a day.

"So who will start the bidding? Do I hear a thousand

dollars?"

John shot up his hand and shouted, "One thousand dollars." The auctioneer looked shocked and several standing near John laughed.

"Are you sure, son?" asked the auctioneer. "You know there's not a racetrack in America that will let you race him."

"I'm sure," said John. "I'm not going to race him. I'm just going to ride him."

The crowd laughed even louder as the slight young man came forward to claim his horse. True, it was short for a thoroughbred but he was still a big horse. He had the best features of a quarter horse in that he could run faster than other horses for short distances but he was also true to his thoroughbred breeding in that John felt he would be faster than any cow pony in Texas. What John saw was a horse that could best any contender and be his partner for many years.

Before John had even paid for the horse he decided on a name: Midnight. His coat was sleek and shiny and as black as coal. John decided the name Midnight suited him.

John could not have been prouder of his purchase. He felt Midnight was the most beautiful horse he had ever seen. He found a saddle shop and bought a saddle and bridle.

Over the next several weeks, John spent every available moment in the saddle riding the countryside outside of New York City. He was amazed at Midnight's speed. One of the first things he realized is he would not need spurs with Midnight. He was very responsive to John's gentle movement in the saddle and with the reins.

Ready to begin his journey west, John wanted to get away from railroads. Although he appreciated what his father had done in building railroads, he felt he would never get a feel for the real west unless he went to where there were no railroads. But the railroads would provide a great service for him over the next few weeks.

To get out west, he didn't want to ride his prize thoroughbred the whole way. So going by train seemed to be the best option. He boarded a train in New York and secured passage for Midnight in one of the stock cars. He didn't like the idea of a high-strung horse having to share space with lesser animals so he arranged for half of a stock car for Midnight. That was a pattern he would follow as he made his way across the nation. He found with virtually unlimited funds and his father's name that he could pretty much have his way on trains. After all, his father had been successful in developing many of the railroads and routes to the west.

John boarded a train that would ultimately connect all the way to San Francisco. He had no plans to go completely across country but thought he would go until he felt the time was right to find some other form of transportation. After several weeks of riding trains and getting off and exploring the countryside, John arrived in Denver. He got off the train because he liked the way the town looked. His intention was to start riding south until he found a town where he could set up practice. In his mind, he had always wanted to go to Texas. He knew there were fewer than five hundred miles of train track in Texas, and most of that was spiraled out around Galveston.

His first order of business was to fit in with the look of other men in the west. That meant he needed to radically change his appearance. All of his clothes, shoes and boots had always been custom made. It was not that he thought store bought clothes were not good enough for him. It was just his family's practice to have a tailor come to their Fifth Avenue home every month and take orders for any new items John or his parents needed. John's mother was always getting him new clothes for every occasion.

On his trip out west, John packed a steamer trunk with

just a few changes of clothes and a few pair of shoes. He quickly realized if he was going to travel by horseback, he would not have room for more than the boots he was wearing and one additional change of clothes. But even as he got rid of the rest of his possessions, he recognized it was not enough just to pare down his wardrobe. He would need completely different clothes.

He visited a small mercantile in Denver and to his surprise and joy he found the proprietor had a good selection of used clothing and boots. John picked out a single pair of jeans, two denim shirts, and a pair of long johns. He found a pair of boots that looked like they had been worn for years.

"How much for this pair of boots?" John asked as he turned them over and inspected the soles.

"Normally that pair of boots would cost three dollars," replied the storeowner. "But as you can see, these boots had new soles put on them not more than two months ago. So I'll take four dollars for them."

"How about the boots I've got on?" asked John. "I'm not going to need them anymore. Will you trade me, my boots for yours?"

The storeowner's eyes grew big as he beheld John's

beautifully crafted custom boots.

"Sure, I guess I would trade you. It looks like your foot is about the same size as mine." John pulled off his boots and the storekeeper put them on and smiled as he felt the soft leather caress his feet.

"You've got a deal, sir. That'll be six dollars for the jeans, shirts, and long johns. And one pair of boots in an even swap." The storeowner smiled as he thought about what a good deal he was making. John put on his new-old clothes and thought that he looked just fine.

John smiled as he realized he not only got the clothes he needed, but he now had the look of someone who had lived his entire life in the west. Looking back at the tailor-made suit and custom shirt he was leaving behind, the owner hurried to try to sweeten his deal.

"I'll be glad to dispose of your old clothes if you would like for me to. No charge." John hesitated and the man added, "And I have this hat that I'll throw in for nothin'. It doesn't look like much and it's pretty stained but it'll keep the sun off of you."

They shook hands and John left the store feeling like he was on his way toward fitting in. No longer did he have the look of a wealthy New Yorker. He looked like an ordinary western cowboy. As he glanced back over his shoulder, John saw the store owner taking off his shirt. He guessed if he came by later, he would see that man dressed in his newly acquired New York tailored suit.

John headed south, stopping in every little town along the way. He was shocked at how backward the towns seemed. Most didn't have any paved streets and commerce was limited to a general store, a couple of saloons, and a few other scattered businesses. He realized none of the towns had a lawyer and most didn't even have a doctor.

When he got to Colorado Springs, he was pleased to find it was a town that already had several lawyers. He could set up practice there but he would be one of several lawyers all after the same business. That might be a place he would like to return to some day but for now he felt he just wanted to get to know more of the west.

Wanting to get more of a taste of western life, John hired on as a hand on a ranch. No one questioned him about his background or much else. He figured since he looked the part of a cowboy, the foreman assumed he was experienced. John realized the old hat he wore was so sweat-stained that it looked as though he had spent many hours laboring in the sun.

Though he had never worked a ranch before, he was a quick study. His horsemanship went a long way to covering the lack of experience in working cattle. He watched the other hands and emulated their movements and what they did with cattle. The work was hard but it suited him. He found he had a knack working cattle. He also enjoyed the long days in the saddle and his association with the other men.

What John realized was, unlike all of the other men he worked with, he had never before earned his own way in life. John's first job in his whole life was on that ranch at age twenty-four. Most of the other men had been working and earning their own way in life since they were twelve or thirteen. The ranch provided him with a place to stay and with his meals as well as feed for his horse. John found he had few other needs. The few dollars he earned each week was enough to provide for any extras he needed. So far that had amounted to purchasing one new shirt, tan in color, that he could wear to church or to the occasional event in town that required that he be more presentable.

On the weekends, John would join the other hands in town for a beer or two. There had not been another time in his life when John had felt more content. He could have spent several years on that ranch and been perfectly happy. But he also felt the pull to move on and explore other towns and find a place where he could practice law.

By the time he got to Pueblo, road dust had covered his clothes and his horse so he rode into town virtually unnoticed. Pueblo was considerably larger than Colorado Springs. He realized he could have a good practice there. But his heart was still set on finding a place where he was truly needed. He was sure there were injustices here but not as many as in smaller towns.

He drifted on through Colorado and down into New Mexico. John stopped in Willow Springs and hired out on another ranch. This time when asked about his experience he stated with confidence that he could handle anything that was required of him on a ranch.

One of the things he realized was he was one of the few men who didn't carry a gun so John bought a saddle gun. It was a Winchester model 1866 Lever-Action Repeating Rifle. The rifle had a fifteen round magazine.

He realized he also needed to learn to use a six-gun. He bought a Colt Peacemaker and was told it was a forty-five caliber six shot revolver. The gun shop owner told him that he had to pull the hammer back to cock the gun for each shot. He showed John how the previous owner of the gun had a taller than normal hammer so he could use his other hand to fan back the hammer for quicker shooting. He demonstrated it several times for John simulating how he would do it if he were practicing a quick draw. John carefully watched the fanning action so that he could duplicate the move later on his own.

He also bought ten boxes of shells while he was in town and began practicing. Each evening after supper, John would ride off about five miles from the ranch and practice with his new guns. He practiced every chance he got until he became a dead shot. He could shoot straight by sighting down the barrel and also became proficient at shooting from the hip.

John noticed at first Midnight was spooked when he fired his six-shooter. Gradually the great stallion grew accustomed to the sound of his pistol. Some of the time John would practice on horseback to help Midnight get comfortable with him shooting from the saddle.

John also practiced with his rifle and drawing his pistol and soon became very quick on the draw, though he hoped he would never need to use that skill. Evening after evening he would practice. He went back to town several times to buy new cartridges. Some evenings he would shoot two boxes of shells—one with his saddle gun and one with his six-gun. After a few weeks, he realized he seldom missed his target whether he was shooting from the hip, doing a quick draw, using his saddle gun, or shooting with either from the back of Midnight when in a dead run.

On one trip into Willow Springs, New Mexico, John watched a knife throwing competition and became fascinated with the speed and accuracy of the contestants. He saw the men throw knives with speed that rivaled that of a quick draw gunman. One of the men drew daggers from scabbards on each forearm as well as two that were on his back beneath his shirt. He saw the man deliver all four knives with only a couple of seconds and hit his target squarely with each one.

He bought himself an inexpensive throwing knife and practiced that afternoon along with his shooting practice. The next day, he rode back into town after work hoping to find the men who put on the knife exhibition. As luck would have it, he found one still in town. John struck up a conversation with the man who was more than happy to share some of his expertise with John. The knife-throwing expert happily sold John a double back scabbard, a scabbard for his forearm, and three perfectly balanced daggers, all razor sharp.

For the next month, John spent every available moment practicing shooting and knife throwing. Often he would shoot then throw his dagger and then shoot again. He became an expert and always hit his target. One of his favorite things was to see how quickly he could empty his six-gun and deliver all three knives. He was ultimately as good as he hoped he could be. And he also knew he needed to continue practicing daily to keep that edge.

* * * * * * *

From Willow Springs, he rode down to Santa Fe. He was pleased to find Santa Fe was a well-established city. It had the culture he missed from back east. But as much as he missed much of the life in New York City as a child and Boston as a young adult, John wanted to find a place that didn't have an attorney but needed one.

In Santa Fe, he found a saddle shop that made some of the most beautiful saddles he had ever seen. The saddle maker custom designed a saddle to fit John's proportions exactly. It was also extremely lightweight. Keeping weight to a minimum, John wanted Midnight to be able to run as fast as possible without being encumbered by things he carried. He then spent several weeks abusing the new saddle so the leather looked well-worn and many years old. He really didn't want to be noticed. And his big horse already drew more attention than he wanted.

From Santa Fe, he turned more to the east as he continued drifting south heading into the Panhandle of Texas. John took a couple more ranching jobs staying about a month on each of them. Each evening he continued his target practice with his six-gun as well as his saddle gun, and also his throwing knives. In every town, he assessed it for the need of a lawyer. He continued to realize while there were many injustices in the west, there didn't seem to be much demand for lawyers.

John traveled down to Fort Worth and found it was a cattle town that had nearly been wiped out by the Civil War but was coming back due to the many cattle drives going through. John liked what he saw and thought about settling down there, but after a few weeks of ranch work, he drifted on south.

He rode down to Austin and was impressed by the city. There was certainly need for attorneys in Austin and there were many of them. He saw many injustices there. While there were also many policemen in the city, it seemed they turned a blind eye toward the brawls in the many saloons. John even witnessed several gunfights. It seemed to him like gunfights were a legal way to get rid of an enemy or competitor while the local policemen largely ignored the gun play. He wondered who was being paid off to get the police to ignore such lawlessness.

As John rode out of Austin, he thought he would surely return someday and help restore order in the city. He didn't know how or when that would happen but felt that it would happen. From there, John went down to San Antonio. He was surprised to find the Alamo was in the center of town. He recalled how Texans and reinforcements from other states had died there in a fight for the independence of Texas. The United States Army had now rented the Alamo as a quartermaster's depot. As much as he liked San Antonio, or San Anton, as the locals called it, he felt he could make a bigger impact in a smaller city.

John heard of a little town about a half day's ride north and west of San Antonio named Bandera. He heard there was a lot of ranch work to be done there and a shortage of hands. There was something about the name Bandera that caused him to think maybe this was the place he had been looking for. Maybe in Bandera, John would be able to make a difference. Perhaps this would be the place where he would be able to hang out a shingle and start a law practice.

Little did John know how Bandera and the people there would change him forever. He didn't know that in Bandera he would make decisions that would alter the course of his life. As he rode on to the little cow town, he believed he was getting ready to embark on an adventure. He just didn't know how big of an adventure was waiting for him.

CHAPTER 11: 1871

John realized the former marshal must have been in cahoots with the town council. How else could such land wealth be explained for a town marshal? He also recognized the council was already taking steps to be able to control John by making him party to the same shady land deals they handed out to Marshal Edwards.

So far, serving as marshal was suiting John fine. He even liked the bit of detective work he was doing now. He still wished he was able to practice the law, but reasoned that keeping the law was also satisfying. All that morning the Scales of Justice in John's head were woefully out of balance. He didn't know how to restore balance, but he was determined to find a way.

John walked to the bank hoping to see Harvey Fowler. As soon as he walked in, he caught sight of the bank owner sitting at a large desk in the back corner. John removed his hat and walked back toward Fowler.

The banker stood and motioned with his hand for John to come on over. John thought he and the judge were using the same tailor for both wore identical suits and ties. The only difference was the slide on the judge's tie was gold and Fowler's was silver inlaid with what appeared to be diamonds. John thought there must be a lot of money in banking.

"Howdy, Marshal. I think this is the first time you've been in the bank. How are things goin' in your new job?"

"Very well thanks," replied John. "Bandera's a great town. And it remains quiet and peaceable for the most part. Some days I feel like I'm not earnin' my salary."

"Don't worry about that, Marshal. You'll be earnin' your money soon enough," replied Fowler.

What an odd thing to say. I wonder what he means by that.

"But even if there is no law-breaking going on, Marshal, you're earnin' your keep. We all feel safer knowin' you're on the job. So tell me how I can help you today?"

"Well Mr. Fowler, I was thinkin' I could use a bank

account. I don't like walkin' around with a lot of money on me," said John.

"So what do you consider a lot of money, Marshal?"

"I've got eighty-seven dollars I saved from when I was working on the H&F."

Fowler had a crooked grin as he said, "My, my, John, that is a lot of money." John could hear a bit of mockery in Fowler's voice. Little did the banker know John had greater wealth than probably anyone in all of Texas. "I think I can get an account open for you. And John, if you would like, I would be glad to arrange for part of your salary to automatically go into your account. I know we are payin' you eighteen dollars a month. By the way, that's two dollars more than we paid Marshal Edwards."

"I didn't know that. Why pay me more than Marshal Edwards?" asked John.

"We talked about it and thought that your quick gun and reputation was worth an extra two dollars to the town. Like I said Marshal, you'll earn it—every cent of it."

There it was again. It was like Fowler had another message he was giving John but John couldn't figure out what that message was.

"So Marshal, would you like for me to have part of your

check deposited in your account each month?"

"I guess so. That would make good sense."

"How much do you think you want to hold out each month?"

John thought about it for a minute and said, "I only need about five dollars a month. The town provides my room and board. I was even surprised that the town paid for room and board for my horse. The only expense I have is for candy from the mercantile and an occasional beer at the Cheer Up."

Fowler said, "Yup, I heard you have a beer most every night and have never had more than two in one night."

John shot him a quick stare. "How'd you—oh yeah. Ms. Hawkins must have told you. A man can't have many secrets in this town."

"Now John," said Fowler, "it's not like that. We just can't help but notice some things about our new marshal. After all, you're already pretty popular in Bandera. We are just proud to have you here."

John knew there was more to it than that. From that moment on, John realized he had to be careful about what he did and what he said. It seemed there was always someone watching. John even wondered if the council had some others in town who fed information to them.

"So John, I'll take care of arrangin' for thirteen dollars of your salary goin' straight to your new bank account. Just think, if you keep saving like that you can put back more than a hundred and fifty dollars a year. Pretty good I think. How many marshals were ever able to do that?"

"Thanks, Mr. Fowler. I guess I need to move on. I like to check on things in town before I make it out to the surrounding ranches."

"Why are you riding out to ranches?" Fowler asked.

"Just tryin' to keep my pulse on things. I mainly focus on those within the town limits. It helps me get to know folks and to keep track of what all's goin' on 'round here."

And with that John turned and walked out of the bank. Back on the boardwalk, he pondered his conversation with the banker. It was obvious the council was keeping close tabs on him. He also realized that having room and board included in his compensation was more about them knowing where he was at all times.

He went around to the livery stable and saddled up Midnight. He wanted to go to the H&F and see Slim. And if he was lucky, he would also get to see Charlotte. But instead of riding south, he purposely rode out north away from the

H&F. He couldn't afford to have the council know he was going to speak to Slim.

By early afternoon, John had visited several of the smaller ranches and visited with a number of the local citizens. He then skirted the town and headed south to the H&F. Midnight got into a gentle lope. John realized it had been a couple of days since he had ridden. He made a pledge to himself and a silent promise to Midnight not to let a day pass without getting into the saddle.

The black horse ran strong and true. John marveled at how he could run without even seeming to get winded. After about an hour, he arrived at the H&F. He rode over to the watering trough, swung down, and let Midnight drink his fill. He then walked Midnight up to the house and looped the reins over the hitching rail, just as Charlotte came through the door to see who had arrived. She was wearing a pale yellow dress that accentuated her figure. She wiped her hands on her apron. Her hair was pulled back into a ponytail.

John removed his hat and said, "Hello, Ms. Charlotte. Is your father here?"

"Hello, Mr. Crudder," replied Charlotte. "Yes, he's here. Come on in. Can I get you a glass of lemonade?"

"That's the best offer I've had all day," said John as he removed his hat and followed Charlotte into the house.

"Here's your lemonade. Daddy's back in the office. Go on back. You know where it is."

"Thanks, Ms. Charlotte," said John as he headed toward the back of the house.

As his boots sounded through the house, he heard Slim call out, "Hello, John. Come on back and set a spell."

John walked in and shook Slim's hand. "Have you got time to talk a bit?"

"Of course," replied Slim. "What's on your mind?" Seeing the serious look on John's face, Slim got up and closed the door to the office. "Sit down, John."

John didn't know quite where to start. "I think you're right. There's much more goin' on in town than it appears. And I think at least some of the town council is involved."

John told about the judge offering to set him up with a ranch that he wouldn't have to pay for. He told about Sally and what she told him about how she got started in business and of the land she owned. John told about his conversation with Clem about Marshal Edwards.

"Now that surprises me," said Slim. "I never would've thought Marshal Edwards would've been mixed up with that bunch."

"Well see, that's the thing. I don't think he was always part of their shenanigans. Accordin' to Clem, he started pickin' up little ranches a couple of years ago. And I think he was wantin' out but didn't know how to get out."

"That makes sense. Edwards had a couple of talks with me tellin' me he suspected there was some dirty business goin' on. He never said what it was or who was involved but I could tell that he wanted me to know. And I think he would have told me but he died before he got a chance."

"And they are already startin' to try and control me. I found out they're payin' me two dollars a month more than they did Marshal Edwards. And then they offered to get me a ranch that I wouldn't need to pay for. He even said that would be a good start like he was planning on gettin' me more land. He also said that the council found out about the good deals and they took turns buyin' them for a bargain. The judge said Sally was gonna give up her turn so I could get the ranch.

"And when I was at the bank, Mr. Fowler said I would be earning my money very soon. I'm not sure what he was talkin' about, but I got the feeling they were expectin' some trouble that I would have to take care of."

Slim thumped his fingers on the desk and took in what John said. After a few moments, he said, "If the council is involved then Marshal Edward's thought about contactin' the Texas Rangers was the best step."

"The problem is," said John, "I don't know what evidence Marshal Edwards had on them. All I've got is I think he had his suspicions."

"That's all right, John. Just be patient, I think before long you will have all of the evidence you need. When you get it just let me know how I can support you. We can't let a handful of crooks milk the town dry. If they're not stopped, there is no tellin' what they'll do next."

"It seems like a number of people have just disappeared," said John.

"Wha'cha mean?" asked Slim.

"Well, Clem talked about Judge Anderson helpin' the Widder Jones. Then it seems the judge bought her ranch and she left town without talkin' to anyone. In talkin' with people in town, it seems it's not unusual, people not telling friends goodbye. Several people have just sold out and left town without talkin' to anyone."

"That may not be all that unusual, John," said Slim.

"Maybe, maybe not," said John. "If someone has spent

years in Bandera, don't you think they would at least tell their neighbors they were leavin'?"

"You're right," said Slim. "I don't know why that hasn't bothered me more. I can think of more than a dozen small landowners who have left Bandera in the past few years that never spoke to anyone but just left town. I guess after the first one, I figured that was just the way it was with people these days."

"One thing you can count on," John said. "I'll get to the bottom of it. This group, whoever is involved, has to be stopped."

"John, I don't think you realize how dangerous these people are," said Slim. "Remember they shot Marshal Edwards in the back in front of many witnesses. They act like they can just do whatever they want to without worryin' about gettin' caught. And if the town council is involved, they're more dangerous than I ever realized."

Slim and John talked on through the afternoon until dusk. When their conversation was over, Slim asked, "Can you stay for supper, John?"

"I'd be pleased to," replied John.

John walked out of the office, through the house, and out onto the porch. Charlotte was sitting in the swing. She smiled and said, "Can you stay for supper, Mr. Crudder?"

"I'd like that, Ms. Charlotte. May I join you on the swing?" John noticed she had let her hair down and had taken off her apron.

She moved her dress and patted the seat of the swing. John smiled and sat down next to Charlotte. They just swung back and forth without talking. Occasionally John stole a glance at Charlotte. Charlotte did her own glancing at John. Finally, John worked up courage and reached for Charlotte's hand.

"That didn't take you as long as I thought it would," giggled Charlotte.

"What do you mean?"

"I've been waiting for you to do that," replied Charlotte. "It seemed after you kissed me at the dance, that you have pulled back in your feelings toward me."

"I didn't mean to. It's just that I've had a lot on my mind. I've been tryin' to get a handle on this new job. I don't know much about marshalin'. It's takin' more of my time than I would've thought."

"I guess that makes sense. So long as you're still interested in me."

"Charlotte, I can say that I have never felt like I feel

with you. And I have never been with another woman. After I've been 'round you, I have a hard time concentratin' on my job. I just walk 'round in a daze."

Charlotte smiled, "I'm glad I have that effect on you."

"You don't understand. I can't work like this. I've been thinkin' it would be a good thing if we didn't see each other as much."

Charlotte removed her hand from John's and stared at him. A tear dripped from her eye and she got up and went in the house. John wasn't sure what he did that was wrong. All he did was try to tell her he liked her and that was causing him trouble concentrating on his job. He wondered why he had never heard how hard it was to talk to women— at least some women. And how was he to know that being honest with Charlotte was going to hurt her feelings?

When John went in for supper, he could tell the atmosphere had changed. Charlotte wouldn't look him in the eye. Slim talked a bit but it was hard for John to add much to the conversation. After supper, Slim asked him if he would like to stay the night, especially since it had been dark for a couple of hours. He thought that sounded like a good idea so he accepted. That would give him a chance to see Jesse and maybe ask him how he had messed things up so badly with Charlotte.

John walked over to the bunkhouse and said howdy to several of the hands. He looked for Jesse but they said he had gone off to Tarpley to work and wouldn't be in until late. A few hours later, when Jesse came riding up, John was sitting on a bench in front of the bunkhouse.

"Little Buddy!" said Jesse, "is that you?" He swung down and shook John's hand.

"Hello, Jesse. Workin' mighty late."

"Little Buddy, wait 'til you hear what I found. You're not gonna believe it. I found signs of more of those rustlers. They've got a…"

Just then, John noticed someone ducking into the shadows beside the bunkhouse. He couldn't tell who it was but he had the feeling someone was listening to their conversation. John put his finger to his mouth so Jesse would stop talking. He motioned to the side of the bunkhouse. When they walked over to see who was there, they found no one. Evidently, whoever it was got an earful and sneaked away.

John walked with Jesse over to the corral as Jesse took care of his horse. Jesse continued in a low voice. "It looks like there are probably a dozen men who have taken up residence on the ranch that was sold last year. No one has been livin' there until now. I slipped up to the window and listened as I heard them talkin' about stealin' cattle from several ranches. They were laughin' and drinkin'. I slipped off before they knew I was there. I need to tell Slim right away."

"Jesse, normally I would agree with you, but we don't know who was listenin' to us a few minutes ago. If they're still around, I wouldn't want them to see you goin' to the house. They would know something was up."

"You're shor right, Little Buddy. I never thought of that."

They returned to the bunkhouse, talked with some of the other hands about life on the ranch, then everyone turned in for the night and someone blew out the lantern. John lay on his bunk contemplating what Jesse had told him. He wondered if the bunch Jesse overheard were connected to what was going on in Bandera. He tossed and turned for a couple of hours and finally drifted off to sleep just before dawn.

John ate breakfast with the hands in the dining hall. He didn't see Slim or Charlotte. He guessed they must have eaten at home. As he ate, he casually looked around at the various tables wondering who could have been listening to his conversation with Jesse. He didn't spot anything suspicious.

After breakfast, he said goodbye to the hands, saddled up Midnight and headed back toward town. He was not in a hurry so he held Midnight to a trot. John wanted to think about what he had learned and what he had told Slim before supper. He wanted to tell Slim what he learned from Jesse but thought he shouldn't risk it right then. The more John thought about it, the more he realized he was in danger and anybody he had contact with was also in danger. That included Charlotte, Jesse, and Slim.

CHAPTER 12: 1871

The judge was the first person he saw as he rode into town. "Hello, Marshal. I hope you're doing well." The judge was walking past the marshal's office on his way to the courthouse. As usual, the judge was dressed in a black suit, bright white shirt, and a black string tie. And as usual, his expensive boots shone with a fresh shine. John wondered if he had Ms. Cora shine his boots after she cooked his breakfast.

"Thanks, Judge Anderson. I'm doin' well. How 'bout you judge?"

"Couldn't be better. I hear you didn't spend the night in town last night."

"How'd you—of course. Sally."

"That Charlotte Hanson is a handsome woman," said the judge.

John's temper flared and he shot the judge a sharp look as he swung down from Midnight. "I don't know what business that is of yours, Judge," John shot back angrily.

"Now simmer down, Marshal, I was just havin' a bit of fun at your expense. No harm meant."

John stomped into the marshal's office. Clem was not there. John checked the jail and realized Clem had already released their prisoner as planned. And knowing Clem, John knew he had released him before breakfast was served. John smiled to himself. It was like Clem was going to have to personally pay for the prisoner's breakfast.

The conversation with the judge continued to circle around in John's head. His anger had subsided. As John thought about it, he nodded to himself. Maybe it was good for the council to think he was out with Charlotte. That would take the focus off his meeting with Slim and Jesse. The last thing John wanted to do was to bring suspicion on the two of them. But he also wondered if there was someone on the H&F that was taking reports back to the council. The more he considered it, the more he thought that could be the case.

John left his office and went on his morning rounds. When he went to the Better Days, he went in and saw Sally was helping pick up the rest of the breakfast dishes. He took off his hat, nodded his head and said, "Ms. Sally."

"Hello, Marshal. I hope you slept well last night."

John felt heat come into his face. "Yes, I had a fine night. Thank you." And with that, he turned and walked out of the hotel. He guessed he was going to have to get used to people snooping into his business. But he didn't see how he was going to be able to ever get used to it. Not only was John a private person, but he knew he could not conduct the investigation into what he was convinced were the secret activities of the town council without bringing suspicion upon himself.

As he continued his rounds, he thought it would be a good idea to pay a visit to the mercantile. He entered and heard a little bell tinkle just as he had when he visited the judge. Seth Davis came out of the back room and said, "Hello, Marshal. I was wondering when you would get around to visiting me."

"Hello, Mr. Davis," said John. "What do you mean by that?"

"I just know you've visited 'bout every business in town except mine. I was wondering when you would make it by here. I didn't mean anything personal," replied Davis.

"I'm sorry, Mr. Davis. I guess I woke up on the wrong side of the bed this morning. I had no call to speak sharply with you."

"That's all right, Marshal. I know the bunkhouse is not nearly as comfortable as your room over at the Better Days."

John was stunned once again how quickly it seemed that other people knew about his business. This time he hid his surprise and said, "You're shor right about that. Mr. Davis, I was thinking that it was about time for me to buy some new clothes. I want to make a good impression as marshal and I've only got three shirts and one of those is my Sunday shirt."

"I can shor help you, Marshal. What did you have'n mind?" asked Davis.

"I was thinkin' of two more shirts, one in denim and maybe one in tan. Do you have anything like that?" asked John.

"I can fix you up. I don't often get to sell two shirts at a time. But Marshal, if you were to buy three shirts, I could make you a really good deal on all three."

John smiled, mostly to himself. "Mr. Davis," said John, "I don't really have that kind of money."

"That's all right, Marshal. I'll be glad to put it on account for you. I know you've put most of your money into the bank."

Once again, John was surprised at how much other people knew about his business. However, he didn't mention this to Davis. He just took it in stride. "Thanks, Mr. Davis, but the two shirts will be enough for me."

"All right, Marshal. I'm not sure what we have in your size. Seems like most of the men around here are bigger—I mean, there's not much call for shirts in your size. No offense."

"No offense taken, Mr. Davis. I've come to terms with my size many years ago. Maybe you have something in boy's sizes that might fit me."

Davis snapped his fingers. "You're right. I do. I should've thought of that myself. I've got lots of shirts for boys." He started rummaging through his stock.

"It won't be the first time I've bought shirts in boy's sizes. I've found they work pretty well."

"Here you go. And John, you can get three boy's shirts

for less than the cost of two men's shirts. Are you sure you wouldn't like to go with three?" Davis asked.

"All right, Mr. Davis," replied John. "It's easy to see you're a good salesman. I'll get three. See if you have a white one as well."

"I do that for sure. And the white ones are only half the price of the colored ones. I could get you two white ones for the price of one."

John smiled and let out a laugh. "Mr. Davis, you're sure a good salesman. I'll do it. But all I'm gonna take is the four of them, even if you have a 'buy five and get one free sale."

"Funny you'd say that," said Davis. "I was just thinkin' of somethin' like that."

John laughed. As he walked out of the store with his purchases, he was struck once again at how much people knew about his business. He walked into the Better Days and saw Sally over behind the counter.

She said, "Well Marshal, it looks like you have been shopping over at Davis Mercantile. Did you get something nice?"

"I just got some shirts," said John. He went up to his room and put his shirts away. John was still seething about the whole town knowing his business. But as he reflected on things, he realized the knowledge of his movements was restricted to the town council. It didn't appear anyone else even cared about where he went or what he did. The council, however, was very interested in everything he did.

Leaving the hotel, John returned to his rounds. He felt it was time to go see the mayor. He walked on past the courthouse and went into the town offices. The mayor was there so John removed his hat and said, "Howdy, Mayor Wright."

"Hello, John. It's good to see you out about town. Anything on your mind or are you just out makin' rounds?" John smiled to himself as he saw the mayor was wearing a suit that looked identical to what the judge and the banker wore. He amused himself wondering if they got a discount by ordering three at a time.

"No nothing special, Mayor, I'm just makin' rounds. How are things goin' with you?"

"Well they're going very well. I'm glad you stopped by. Come on back into my office. I have some business to discuss with you."

That surprised John a bit. He followed the mayor back to his office. "Have a seat, John. I've got a stack of work waitin' here for you." John didn't know what work the mayor could have for him. As far as he knew, his job was to patrol the town, prevent crime, and arrest lawbreakers. What else could the mayor have?

He didn't have to wait long to find out what the mayor had on his mind. "There's a stack of papers that need to be served."

"I didn't realize that was part of my job," said John. "Just tell me what to do and I'll get it done."

"Well John," continued the mayor, "the rest of the council gets all of their paperwork over to my office once a week so you can pick it all up here each Wednesday morning. We have a two week backlog now so there is a lot of extra work for you to do at first just to get caught up."

"What kind of papers are you talkin' about?" asked John.

"Harvey always has several people who are past due on a mortgage or a note. Sometimes there is an eviction that you need to handle. Gideon always has subpoenas that need to be served for the court. Then there's Sally. When she has a deadbeat who won't pay, it's your job to get them to pay up or you arrest them. And Betsy is always having some cowboys breakin' up her place. Every Monday mornin', she prepares a list of what was broken and who broke it. Mostly that comes from cowboys on the ranches out-of-town that come in on the weekend and get liquored up. You get to ride out and collect from them."

John was remembering Mr. Fowler saying he was going to be earning his salary. Suddenly John realized being marshal in Bandera was not nearly as easy as he thought. But still he didn't mind it. In fact, he would like being busy a lot more than he liked just walking around town trying to look busy.

"Then there's Seth at the mercantile. He has a long list of people who owe him money but haven't paid. When they are three months in arrears, if they can't pay, you are empowered by the town council to collect any way you can. If that means takin' a horse or cattle or just puttin' the fear of God into them so they will pay their bills, that's your job."

"But what if they really can't pay?" asked John.

"We're patient to a point," said the mayor. "But people have to realize they have to keep their commitments. Business people can't run on charity. They're in business to make money. It is an honest livin' and they deserve to get paid for their merchandise and their services.

"Then there is the subject of taxes. Marshal, you're also

the chief tax collector. And we have lots of farmers and ranchers who are delinquent. Unfortunately, some of them will eventually need to be evicted because they either can't or won't pay."

"This sure gives me a different view of things," said John. "I had no idea the marshal had to do all of that. But if it's my job, I'm glad to do it. I'm all about upholdin' the law."

"Now I'm gettin' to the best part. John, you're gettin' paid extra for all of these additional duties. And don't worry, it is all legal and above board. You can check with any other lawmen. They'll tell you the same thing. Here's how it works. You get two dollars any time you have to serve papers. When you make an arrest, you get five dollars. Any time you evict someone there is five dollars extra for you. On top of that, we pay by the mile for all of your riding. Once a month, you submit an estimate of how many miles you have ridden. It's an honor system. You get five cents for every mile. That alone brings in an extra thirty dollars or so each month. At least it did for Marshal Edwards.

"Oh yes," continued the mayor. "You're also paid ten percent of any taxes or other collections you make. Most of the past five years, Marshal Edwards earned an extra four thousand dollars. So, as you can see, there's a lot of opportunity to make extra money. And the more you want to work, the more money you can make. Why Marshal, it wouldn't surprise me if you could make over five thousand dollars a year just doing your job. What do you think about that?"

John was stunned. He had no idea there was that much money being paid to marshals. And it was not under the table but was legal and above board. He knew it was legal for he had learned about this practice while he was in law school.

"Mayor, I just don't know what to say. That's more money than anyone in town makes except say for the council."

"You're probably right about that," said the major. "And don't you worry 'bout the council. We do just fine." He didn't add anything else but left it to John's imagination to guess what he meant.

John said his goodbyes and went back to the marshal's office with a stack of papers. He sat down and started sorting them into piles; subpoenas, back taxes, bank collections, other business collections. As he was sitting there, Clem walked in and saw him going through the stack of papers.

"Oh good," said Clem. "I can see you went to see the mayor. You picked up the papers for this week and, I guess, judging from the size of the stack, last week's too. So, you gonna divide them up now or later?"

"You mean you knew about this?" asked John.

"Oh yes," said Clem. "Marshal Edwards would always divide them with me. Some months I got more than he got. Of course, he pays me half as much as the council pays him."

"So you mean I make money on papers you serve?" asked John.

"You bet," said Clem. "That's why it's so good to be the marshal. But it's not too bad being the deputy. I made an extra two thousand dollars last year! And that's in addition to the hundred fifty dollars salary they pay me."

John once again found himself speechless. It was not that anything was illegal here but he found it amazing that the marshal and deputy had made so much money in the past. If this were widely known, John thought there would be a line of people applying to get the jobs.

Suddenly, they heard shots fired.

CHAPTER 13: 1871

J ohn and Clem rushed out to the street and saw people pointing at the bank. Fearing a bank robbery, John and Clem ran toward the bank and took up positions beside the doors. Then John crept around in time to see Harvey Fowler standing over a man lying on the floor. Fowler raised his hand and shot the man in the chest with a Remington Double Derringer. The gun made a hole about two inches away from another red rimmed hole in the fallen man's chest.

"Harvey," said John. "What's goin' on here?"

"This yahoo came in and shouted somethin' at me. The next thing I knew he was pullin' his gun. If I hadn't've got the drop on him, he would have killed me. Look at the bullet hole in the wall above my chair."

John put his six-gun away and checked on the bullet-ridden man. "Looks like he's dead. Somebody go get the doc. He'll have to certify he's dead."

"Well I can tell you that, Marshal," offered Clem. "He's dead!"

"The doc is also the coroner. He's the only one who can legally declare someone is dead," said John, drawing on his law school education.

"We ain't never done that before," said Clem. "We just call the undertaker and he puts 'em in a box."

"Clem, just go get doc," said John with exasperation.

"Harvey," John said. "Start at the beginning and tell me what happened."

"I've already told you. Ol' Thompson came in here shoutin' and threatenin' me."

"Thompson?" asked John. "Who is he?"

"Frank Thompson," said Harvey. "He was behind on his note. He's on your list. You're supposed to have collected from him."

"How much did he owe you?" asked John.

"Thirty-seven dollars an' it was due last week. He knew I was gonna swear out a warrant for his arrest if he didn't pay by Friday."

"So why'd you shoot him again?" John asked as he scratched his head.

Harvey said, "To make sure he was dead. I didn't want him to shoot at me again."

The doc walked in grumbling and said, "What's all this foolishness about declaring someone dead?" He looked down at the man on the floor and said, "He's dead." And with that he turned and left the bank in a huff. One of the tellers laughed and then quickly ducked his head as John shot him a piercing stare.

When Clem got back, John said, "Clem, please take care of this man the way you normally would."

"You mean call the undertaker and put 'em in a box?"

"Yup."

"Mr. Fowler, I'll need you to come by the marshal's office later today. I'll write up what you said and then I'll need you to sign it."

"Marshal," said Fowler. "What's that about? We've never done it that way before."

"Well, we're doing it that way now!" With that, John turned around and left the bank. All the way back to his office, John couldn't get rid of the picture in his mind of

Harvey standing over Thompson and coldly putting a bullet in his chest. He didn't think Harvey was in the wrong. He had a right to defend himself but Thompson looked pretty dead from the first bullet. But there was something about Harvey's expression when he pulled the trigger. John thought he looked like a cold-blooded killer.

Instead of going to his office, he turned and went up to the judge's house. As he walked in, Cora responded to the tinkle of the bell.

Removing his hat John said, "Hello, Ms. Cora. Is the judge in?"

"He sure is, Marshal. He said if you come by to send you on into his office. He's expecting you."

John knocked on the judge's door and was bidden to enter.

"Well Marshal, another visit so soon?"

"Cora said you were expectin' me. How come?"

"It's simple, Marshal. I heard the shots from over around the bank. I figured you'd be by before long. You want to tell me what happened?"

John went through the events at the bank. He said what Fowler told him and also how he saw Fowler put an extra hole in Thompson's chest.

"Are you saying he broke the law? Harvey was defending himself. And it sounds like he may have even just shot a dead man," said the judge.

John realized the judge and Harvey went back a long way together. He changed his tack. "No, it was just a bit unusual to see a banker shoot someone."

"Harvey's a good shot," said the judge. "We quail hunt together. He's a dead shot with anything he picks up. One day when we were hunting, Harvey had already emptied both barrels of his shotgun when he flushed another quail. Harvey pulled out his derringer and brought down the quail. And he didn't tear up the meat either. He put the shot right through the quail's head."

"It's a good thing he was quick with his derringer today or he might have been killed," said John.

"I wouldn't worry about Harvey, Marshal. This's not the first scrape he's been in and I know it won't be the last," added the judge.

"Thanks, Judge," said John. "This is the first shootin' since I've been marshal. I just needed to talk to someone. Thanks for listenin'."

The judge stood and came around his desk and put his hand on John's shoulder as he ushered him out of his office.

"Glad to do it, Marshal. You come by any time."

John left the office, put his hat on and walked slowly back to the office. After walking a few steps, he turned and looked back at the judge's house. As he did, he saw a face pull back from the window and the curtain ruffle.

Returning to the office, John again thought about watching the banker shoot Thompson. The judge was wrong about Fowler not breaking the law. Clearly he was guilty. If not of murder, then manslaughter or at least desecrating a dead body. But he also knew no jury in this town would convict him given the circumstances.

John wanted to tell Slim what he saw but also knew it was not safe for him to go out to the H&F. He would wait until Slim was in town and find a way to talk to him without being seen together. Or perhaps he could send a letter to him by one of the ranch hands when he saw one in town.

About noon, John went over to the Better Days for dinner. Sally was there as usual. "Hello, Marshal," said Sally. "Sounds like there was some excitement in town this morning."

John had a seat and Sally joined him. Almost immediately someone placed a plate of steak and potatoes in front him. "Will you be eating, Ms. Sally?" asked the young waitress.

"No, I'm just visiting with the marshal for a bit." Sally continued, "They tell me that was the first shootin' you've had since becomin' marshal."

"Word does get around in this town fast," said John.

"Well, it's a small town, Marshal," said Sally. "We have shootin's from time to time. It pays for a body to know how to shoot." She reached into her apron pocket and pulled out a Remington Double Derringer that looked identical to the banker's.

She laughed as she saw John's eyes get big.

"If I was you, Marshal, I'd get one of these too. All of the council carries 'em. And we are all crack shots. Marshal Edwards carried one as well and he was a dead shot. But then again, I don't guess you need one. We've all heard of the dagger you keep up your sleeve."

John looked surprised. But so far, no one knew that he kept two more daggers in the scabbards on his back.

"There are not many secrets in this town, Marshal," said Sally. "That is unless we really wanted to keep one. Then we can be rather tight-lipped." She nodded to John and stood up. "I'll let you finish your dinner."

John wondered what secrets Sally was referring to. It

was as though she wanted to include him in the secrets. He pondered this and thought it was a veiled invitation to join the council in whatever they did in secret. The more he thought about it, the more convinced he was that he needed to find out what was going on in this town.

He felt the key was to see if he could find out what went on at council meetings. He had heard them talk about their monthly meetings but as far as he knew, he had never found out when they met. And he knew they never met during the day. John checked the calendar and found it was the first of the month.

John thought the first of the month was likely the day the council would meet. But where would the meeting take place? Then he thought of the spaciousness of the judge's office. Yes, that was likely where they'd meet. But when? It was then that John decided it was going to be a long night.

That evening, he made his rounds as usual and then went by the saloon for his nightly beer. He visited with several of the cowboys who were at the bar. Betsy was refilling mugs when she got to John. "Marshal, can I pour you another?"

"No, Ms. Betsy," replied John. "I'm tuckered out. I'm gonna turn in early." John said his goodbyes and left the saloon and walked next door to the hotel.

Sally was walking through the lobby. He tipped his hat and greeted her.

"Goin' to your room so soon, Marshal?"

"It's late for me. I've had a long day," said John. "I'm gonna turn in now. I guess I'll see you at breakfast."

"You shor will, Marshal."

John walked on to the top of the stairs and went down the hall to his room that was in the back corner. He lit his lamp and put it close to the window so it would be well seen from the outside. After about twenty minutes, he blew out the lamp and crept out of his room. He was fortunate his room was next to the back stairs. As he opened the door, he was careful no one saw him slip out.

He carefully walked down the stairs and slipped into the shadows behind the hotel. He waited a few minutes for his eyes to adjust to the dark and then started off toward the judge's house. Moving silently, he crept from building to building. The only sounds in town were coming from the saloon. He could hear the piano playing and a few cowboys laughing loudly.

Finally, he got to the judge's house and recognized the window to the judge's office on the back corner. The window was open and there were several lamps lit. Peeking inside, John saw the judge sitting at his desk drinking whiskey. It looked to him like the judge was waiting for others.

John backed up and slipped around the corner of the next building and waited. He hoped he was right that a council meeting would take place tonight. He waited for what he thought was more than two hours. Occasionally, he would look in the judge's office window and confirm that the judge was still there. Each time he looked, he saw the judge was still sipping his whiskey and waiting.

He returned to his perch and settled in. After another half hour, John heard the front door of the judge's house open. He heard Betsy call out and the judge answer her and bid her to join him in the office. Judging by the stars, John guessed it was close to midnight.

"Howdy, judge. Got any whiskey?" asked Betsy.

"You know I do. I always buy the best reserve stock you've got."

Betsy giggled and filled her glass. As she did, John heard Sally call out from the front door.

"We're in here," Betsy called back.

One by one, the other council members joined in the

next few minutes. As they gathered, they all partook liberally from the judge's fancy crystal decanter. It was easy to see they were long-time friends. They laughed and drank for a while and then started to settle in to get ready for their meeting.

After a while the judge said, "All right, everyone take a seat and we'll get started." John moved quietly until he was beneath the window. He waited and then the judge said, "I guess the main order of business tonight is the marshal. How is he settling in?"

Harvey said, "Well you know he came to the bank today when Mr. Thompson came in shootin'. He seemed to take exception to the fact that I put an extra hole in Thompson."

"It's a good thing Thompson was not a better shot," said Sally.

"I wasn't worried," said Harvey. "I saw him when he entered the bank. I pulled my derringer and was ready when he came toward the back. I already had my gun on him when he went for his six-gun. My problem was deciding where I wanted to shoot him. I wanted to put one between his eyes, but Betsy, I was remembering how much that cowboy bled that you shot in the head. I didn't want my rug getting messed up."

They all laughed. Seth Davis asked, "Do you think the marshal's a problem?"

"Not at all." Sally sipped her whiskey. "I see him every day and get to talk to him more than most. He's got questions from time to time but he is not suspicious. I think he will be joinin' us before long."

"Well, I'm not so sure." The judge wrinkled his brow. "I offered to set him up with the Jenkins' place. He didn't want any part of it. Said he needed to concentrate on his job. We'll just have to see how he handles himself."

"By the way, what'd you do with the Jenkins?" asked Mayor Wright.

"I shot 'em both," Sally said as if she did something like that every day, "and had Hank bury them in the ravine a few miles east of town."

"I didn't think we were putting anyone else there." Betsy voiced her concern. "Isn't it getting crowded?"

"There's still room," Sally responded. "I rode out there with Hank when we hired him and told him where to bury people should the need arise. I made sure he knew he was supposed to keep track of where he dug and only move further east and never go the other way."

John couldn't believe what he was hearing. Not only

was the council involved in theft but they were all murderers. How could such a gang of crooks get control of an entire town?

"Gideon," asked Seth, "did Marshal Edwards get off the telegram to the Texas Rangers like he threatened?"

"No. The old fool tried to send it from here in town. I was alerted immediately. If he had gone to San Anton, we would never've known if he sent a telegram or not. But even if he had gotten a telegram off, our man on the Rangers would have intercepted it. And don't forget we also have our man in the governor's office. I think we couldn't be safer."

The group laughed. Judge Gideon got up and passed the decanter of whiskey. Everyone seemed in good spirits. And why not? They were untouchable.

"I sure hated losin' Johnson," said Betsy. "He was our troubleshooter for three years. He never did get greedy like his predecessors."

"It's just as well," said Harvey. "I never like keeping a troubleshooter that long. There is just too big of a risk to us. Crudder really did us a favor when he shot him at the dance."

"I thought it was too big of a risk getting Johnson to murder Edwards in public," said Seth.

"It all worked out all right," said the judge. "We got rid of Edwards and Johnson at the same time and even got a new marshal to boot."

"Let's get back to Crudder," said Mayor Wright. "I don't like him goin' out to the H&F. What do you think he talked to Slim about?"

"According to Cody and Gus, he was just there to see Charlotte," said Harvey. "They said he spent the night in the bunkhouse. He talked to Jesse out behind the bunkhouse. They were out there a long while and when they came back in, Gus said Jesse had a troubled look in his eyes."

"So do you think John told Jesse about some suspicions?" asked the judge.

"I'm afraid it might be the other way around," said Harvey. "Gus said Jesse was out at Tarpley that day. He might have come across the men who are runnin' our cattle operation. But the good thing is that none of those men know who they're workin' for. As far as they know, they are workin' for Cody and Gus."

The council members smiled and nodded together.

"That's good," said the judge. "But that also means Jesse is now a problem. Cody and Gus will be in town tomorrow to get their assignments since it's Saturday.

Harvey, when they come to the bank to make a deposit, tell 'em to take care of Jesse."

As John listened, he couldn't believe what he was hearing. Not only had they murdered many others but it sounded like they were going to kill Jesse next. Somehow, he needed to get word to Jesse and maybe even Slim.

John slipped back into the shadows and made his way to his room. He wanted to be in the hotel before the meeting broke up, just in case Sally was suspicious and came to see if he was in his room. He quietly ascended the back stairs and went into his room.

He hadn't been there long when he saw a shadow beneath his door.

CHAPTER 14: 1871

J ohn started breathing heavily as though he were asleep. He even did a bit of snoring, being careful not to overdo it. After a few minutes, the shadow moved on. John realized Jesse was not safe and perhaps his own life was also at risk.

The next morning, John made his rounds as usual. He saw several members of the council and they were friendly as they had been previously. John thought it was important to start working through the stack of papers from the mayor. He served a half dozen subpoenas and delivered delinquent tax notices to four of the small ranchers. John couldn't help but think that some of them would end up disappearing and being buried. He shuddered at the thought.

Toward dusk, John headed Midnight back toward town. On his way, he couldn't help but go by the ravine that served as the burial ground for those who got in the way of the council. The ground showed a lot of recent activity and evidence of digging in more than two dozen places. Only about half a dozen were fresh. The others looked to be a month old and some of them perhaps years old. It was obvious someone had taken pains to cover the digging activity and to erase tracks. John thought he better get a branch and wipe out his own tracks as well.

When he got back to town, he dismounted Midnight in front of his office, and took a handful of papers from his saddlebag. Mayor Wright was walking down the boardwalk and called, "Evenin' Marshal. You're out mighty late."

"Like you said, I have some catching up to do with the backlog of paperwork. I got all the subpoenas served and delivered a bunch of the delinquent tax notices. Funny thing; the small land owners who got the notices seemed surprised that they owed any taxes. And most of them also seemed scared right out of their skin. It's good to see citizens taking the law seriously." John laid it on thick hoping to buy him enough time to figure out what to do next.

"That's fine, Marshal," said the mayor. "That will make your next paycheck a nice one."

"It shor will. This job is turnin' out to be better than I thought. The more I think about it maybe I'll be able to get me a small spread soon."

"I'll keep my eye out for you, Marshal," said the mayor. "'Course the Jenkins' place is already taken but there are little places comin' available all the time. In fact, as you serve the delinquent tax notices, take a look at the land. You might find somethin' that's to your likin'. More than likely most of those places will come on the market sooner or later. More than likely sooner."

"I'll do that, Mayor." John took the papers into his office and then led Midnight over to the livery stable. After giving him water and oats, he began to groom him. Ever since his first horse, he found grooming a horse brought him pleasure. It was relaxing and helped him put away the troubles of the day. Midnight lifted his head and cocked it toward the door.

A split second later, John heard the report of pistols. He ran out of the livery and saw people gathering around the door of the saloon. John ran as fast as he could and pulled his six-gun as he got to the door. He peered over the swinging doors and saw Jesse lying in a pool of blood. Cody and Gus were on either end of the bar with their guns out. Betsy was behind the bar. It looked as if only the three of them were there when Jesse was shot.

"Hold it right there, Cody. You too, Gus. Get your hands up." John took steps toward them.

Cody said, "Hey John, you know us. It's not like that. Jesse got drunk and pulled a six-gun on us. We had to defend ourselves."

"That's right, Marshal," said Betsy. "It's just as Cody said."

"Jesse doesn't even carry a gun," said John.

"Well he had one today," said Gus as he pointed to a gun on the floor near Jesse's body.

"I told you to put your hands up. You're both under arrest," said John.

Gus said, "I'm not gonna hang for this." And he rapidly turned his gun on John. But John was faster. He pumped two shots into Gus as he fanned the hammer. Then with his left hand, he reached up the sleeve of his gun hand and grasped his dagger as he dropped to the floor and turned toward Cody. As he suspected Cody had a bead on him.

John let the dagger fly catching Cody in the notch of his

neck, just above the sternum. The dagger was buried to the hilt. Betsy never moved from where she was standing. She let out a gasp as she watched John's knife work. Even though she had heard John was handy with a knife, she had never imagined anyone could throw a knife that fast and with such accuracy.

John became aware of people coming in to the saloon from the street. "I want to know who all witnessed what happened here," asked John.

Several men put up their hands. "We saw 'em challenge you, Marshal. You didn't have no choice. And we ain't never heard of nobody who could throw a knife like that."

"Which of you were in the saloon when Jesse was shot?" The cowboys turned to each other and shook their heads.

Betsy said, "There was no one else here but Cody, Gus, and Jesse."

"That's kind of a small crowd for a Saturday night, isn't it?"

"It's early yet. This place doesn't get lively for a couple more hours. Hands come in from the surrounding ranches but they usually have to put in a day of work before they come to town."

John nodded his head, "I guess that makes sense. Betsy, I need you to write down everything you saw and bring it by my office tomorrow. And you men who saw the second shooting, I need you to sit down right now and write out what you saw. And if you can't write, tell it to me and I'll write it out and let you make your mark."

Just then Clem came running into the saloon. "Marshal, what happened? Is that Jesse? Doggone, ol' Jesse can't be dead."

"I'm afraid he is," said the marshal.

"Do you want me to go get doc so he can pronounce these three dead?" asked Clem.

"No, don't bother doc. Just get on over to the undertaker and tell him we have some more business for him."

"I know that will make him happy. Four dead in two days. That may be a new record for Bandera." Clem turned and walked out of the saloon.

When John had taken each witness's statement, he helped Betsy straighten up the upturned chairs and he bought a beer. John felt a great weight on his shoulders and a deep emptiness. It was an emptiness he knew beer and food wouldn't fill. He had lost the closest friend he had ever had. And it happened at the hands of two men who only a couple of days before he would have considered his friends.

John drank his beer slowly. He listened to stories the men told about Jesse from years gone by. It was as though they had an unofficial wake that night right there in the saloon. John took comfort in the stories. He realized he had let his beer get warm and it wasn't even half gone. He put a dime on the bar and said his goodbyes. As he walked next door to the hotel, he realized the council would likely have another meeting tonight to assess the situation.

He went into his room and, as he did the night before, lit his lamp and placed it on the table by the window. After half an hour, he put out the lamp and lay down on his bed. He had no intention of going to sleep. He figured there was likely no need to go to his hiding place until just before midnight.

He slipped out of his room and down the back stairs, just as he did the night before. John crept from building to building until he came to the quiet place just around the corner from the judge's office. As he suspected, the judge's lamps were lit and his window was open a few inches. He didn't have to wait long. Seth was the first to arrive followed by Betsy and Sally, who walked in together. Then the mayor and bank owner arrived together.

As they assembled, they got right down to business. Evidently the whiskey was only passed around when they were having their regular monthly meeting.

"Betsy," said the judge, "tell us what happened. We've all heard several versions of the story."

She began, "Cody and Gus brought Jesse into the saloon just as we planned. I had kept the doors locked until they got there. I didn't think we wanted any witnesses."

"Good thinkin'," said the mayor.

"Anyway, I locked the door behind them and Cody went to the far end of the bar while Gus was buyin' Jesse a beer. After Jesse drank about half his mug, Cody pulled his gun and called out to Jesse. When Jesse turned, Cody shot him twice. Then Gus shot him twice more for good measure. Cody pulled out the extra gun he brought and threw it down by Jesse. Gus poured the rest of Jesse's beer on him just to make sure the story of him getting drunk would stick. I unlocked the door and ran back behind the bar."

"So what happened next?" asked Seth.

"About then the marshal came runnin'. He challenged

Cody and Gus and told them to raise their hands. When he said he was gonna arrest them, Cody said he wasn't gonna get hung for shootin' Jesse. He turned his gun on the marshal but the marshal shot him twice before Cody could even aim. Then he dropped to the ground and I think that caused Gus to hesitate. Next thing I knew the marshal came up with a dagger that must have been up his sleeve and threw it quicker than anything I have ever seen."

"How did he do that while holding a gun?" asked the judge.

"Well see, that's the thing. He handled his gun with his right hand and threw the dagger with his left. I've never seen anything like it," said Betsy.

"I guess that means we better talk about getting rid of the marshal," said the judge.

But the mayor chimed in, "No, I don't think so. The marshal has really come around. He was out until late servin' papers all across the town and even on several of the outlyin' ranches. He talked about how his next paycheck was gonna be much nicer. And he even said he was thinkin' about becomin' a land owner now that he could afford it."

With that, the conversation got lighter. The judge said, "Then I think that calls for a drink. Who will join me?"

Each of the unholy six filled their glasses and toasted to their success and cleverness.

John used the opportunity to slip back to his room. He got his door closed and his boots off when he heard someone skulking down the hall. John watched beneath his door as the shadow once again stopped. He started his deep breathing and let out a snore or two. In only a few seconds, the shadow moved on.

As he lay there, he knew he had to get out of town and do it now. The Scales of Justice in his head were completely lopsided. But he also realized there was nothing he could do about it. He couldn't get outside help because the council had reinforcements on the state level. John knew if he tried to contact anyone outside of Bandera, he risked tipping his hand. He could not afford that if he valued his life. And after losing his parents and Jesse, he counted life as precious.

CHAPTER 15: 1871

The next morning, John went down to breakfast as usual. Sally came over and without invitation sat down across from the marshal.

"Good mornin', Marshal."

"Mornin', Ms. Sally."

"I was sorry to hear about Jesse getting killed," said Sally.

"Thank you. He was a good man and the best friend I've ever had," said John.

"What do you suppose happened?" asked Sally.

"I can't figure it out," John said wistfully. "I knew Jesse had a temper. I've seen him get set off and want to fight everyone near him. It wouldn't have surprised me to see him fight a whole saloon full of people. But I just can't figure him carrying a gun. I don't know what he was thinkin'."

"I guess we'll never know."

"You're right," John continued eating and nodded to Sally. "I'd better get goin'. I've got a lot of papers to serve today. It was nice visitin' with you, Ms. Sally."

John stood up, dipped his head to Sally, and walked out the door. He turned toward the marshal's office and walked swiftly there. He passed the mayor and greeted him and walked on to the office.

When Clem walked in, John told him that he was leaving him in charge for the day.

"How come?" asked Clem. "Where you goin'?"

"I'm gonna spend the day serving papers," John replied. "There are several of these that are spread out all over the county. I 'spect I'll be gone most of the day."

"You can depend on me, Marshal," said Clem. "I'll take care of everythin' 'round here."

"Thanks, Clem." John walked down to the livery stable and saddled Midnight. He led him over to the hitching rail in front of the office. He went inside and gathered up a big stack of paper work and made a show of loading his saddlebags.

John saw the mayor walking out of the courthouse. He told him he was out to serve more papers.

"'Bout the only way I know to get caught up is just to devote a full day here and there. I ought to get a lot of these cleared up today," John said as he buckled his saddlebag.

John rode out of town to the west so as not to give away his true direction. Once he was out of sight of Bandera, he turned southeast toward San Antonio and urged Midnight into a run. He knew it would take him all day. San Antonio was about fifty miles away. He really hated to put Midnight through that kind of a hard day but he didn't see that he had any choice.

Over the next several hours, John would alternate between a fast lope and a gallop. He realized Midnight would rather gallop than travel at any other speed. Every few minutes, he would give Midnight his head and let him run at full speed. Then he would pull him back into a lope or a trot.

There were several watering holes on the way. John took advantage of all of them, but was careful not to let Midnight drink too much.

John arrived in San Antonio just before noon and went

immediately to the telegraph office and wrote out a message for Mr. Hastings.

To: Howard Hastings, Fifth Ave., New York City

Send telegram to me tomorrow in Bandera. Request I come home immediately. Mother dying. Must join father.

John

John paid for the telegram and waited while it was being sent. He then went back out to Midnight and mounted up. Midnight was anticipating the return trip and started to gallop before John cleared town. He slowed him into a lope until he was clear of buildings, then Midnight resumed his effortless gallop. John knew Midnight was fast and tireless but he never realized what an amazing animal he was until that day.

After a couple of hours, John dismounted and walked Midnight. He knew Midnight could keep running but he didn't want to completely exhaust him. Back in the saddle, John kept Midnight down to a fast lope. It seemed the horse could run at this pace endlessly without lathering up.

John arrived in Bandera at dusk and led Midnight over to the livery stable. He spent the next hour grooming him. Midnight seemed to really enjoy being curried. Several times, he would nuzzle John and whinny. He laughed at his horse and thought he was almost human. It was as though he was saying, *I had fun today. How 'bout you?*

He carried his saddlebags back to the office and told Clem he could go on home and serve papers the next day. He then stacked the papers back into a pile beneath those he had served the day before.

Back at the hotel, John was able to relax. He was pleased he had not missed supper. Sitting by himself, he reflected on the marathon of a ride he had been on. As he thought about how tired he was, he couldn't help but think that Midnight must be exhausted. But he also knew his horse didn't appear to be that tired. He marveled at his wonder horse.

After supper, he went next door to the Cheer Up and had a beer. He visited with Betsy and a few of the cowboys. It seemed everyone was careful not to bring up the shooting of the night before. That was fine with John.

As John lay down to sleep, he contemplated his next move. He knew he was not going to be able to bring justice to Bandera while he was marshal. It didn't look like there was anyone John could call on to address the problems of the town.

John was still angry over the murder of Jesse. He knew

he was going to have to restore balance to the Scales of Justice himself. He wasn't sure how or when but he swore to himself that every member of the council would pay with their lives.

When morning came, John went down to breakfast and was just beginning to eat when Clem walked in."

"Marshal, the telegraph operator just brought this over for you," said Clem as Sally walked over to see what was going on. John opened the envelope and quickly read as he put on his best performance of looking shocked and stricken with fear.

He dropped the telegram on the table and lowered his head. Clem picked up the telegram and read it to Sally.

To: John Crudder, Bandera, Texas

URGENT. Mother at death's door. Come home immediately.

Dad

John walked out of the hotel and made a show of sitting on the bench on the boardwalk. He put his head in his hands and waited. He conjured up the feelings he had when he found out his parents were killed. He wept real tears again today at that memory.

It wasn't long before Sally came out to see if he was all right. The mayor came walking over to see what was going on. When he got there, Sally handed him the telegram. The mayor read it and said, "I'm sorry, John. This is a tough blow."

"I've got to go back to New York. But then there's so much work here that needs to be done," said John.

"Don't worry about things here. Clem can take care of the marshal responsibilities," the mayor said.

"When you see Slim and Charlotte," added John, "please tell them I'm sorry I didn't get to say goodbye. And tell them I hope to see them again someday."

"You don't think you're coming back?" asked the mayor.

"I don't know. Depends on my dad. He's the one who's been in poor health. I'll have to take care of him after...." John's voice dropped and he wiped his eyes.

"John, come over to my office before you leave," said the mayor. "I'll pay you for your time so far."

John went to his room packed a couple of shirts in his bedroll. When he got down stairs, Sally had a sack of food. "It's just some biscuits, ham, and bacon," said Sally. "Maybe it will get you down the road a piece."

"Thanks, Ms. Sally," said John as she leaned over and kissed him on the cheek.

John went to the livery stable and saddled Midnight and walked him over to the mayor's office.

"Come in, John," said the mayor. "I'm real sorry that you have to go but I understand. I was lookin' forward to great things for you in Bandera."

"Thank you, Mayor," said John. "Please tell the council goodbye for me. And tell them that I'll think of them often. I'm sure my life is gonna be different in the future because of my association with the six of you." John knew what he said was true. His life was going to be on a new track thanks to the council.

"That's right nice of you to say," said the mayor. "Here's fifty dollars. That's a bit more than you've earned. Just consider it a little bonus. I also took the liberty of going to the bank and getting Harvey to withdraw the money from your account."

"Thanks, Mayor." John took the money as he shook his hand.

John mounted Midnight and got into a gentle lope and left town to the northeast. As he rode out of town, he thought about what he was going to do next. He knew he was the only one who could right the wrongs in Bandera. He also knew he had to let some time pass before he came back to town.

CHAPTER 16: 1871

Austin is about one hundred and twenty miles from Bandera. John thought about fifty miles a day would be a good pace. If anyone was following him, they would know he was in a hurry but they wouldn't know that, with Midnight's phenomenal speed and endurance, he was actually moving slowly.

The days of riding and nights looking at the stars gave John a lot of time to think. There were six people he had marked for execution. Their time would come. In the meanwhile, he would see what else he could do with his life. He was determined to do his best to blend in and keep his identity a secret. If he could live in the shadows, he would have a chance to balance the Scales of Justice in a way he couldn't do as a lawman or as an attorney.

John thought about Mayor Farley Wright and how he ran the town to suit himself and banker Harvey Fowler and the cold-blooded way he murdered a man, doing so in a way that allowed him to go unpunished. He shuddered as he recalled how mild-mannered Sally Jenson ran her hotel as a seemingly gentle woman, but was in reality the director of the council's private cemetery and had murdered a man and his wife because she wanted their land.

He arrived in Austin after about two and a half days of travel and went to the telegraph office. He sent a message to Mr. Hastings.

Howard Hastings, Fifth Ave., New York City
Will be moving around for a while. Please send ten thousand
dollars to me in Austin, Texas.

He didn't sign the telegram for he knew Mr. Hastings would know who sent it. Mr. Hastings was managing his investments and accounts. John knew he could depend on him to watch out for his interests. John didn't have any particular plans for the money but he wanted to have enough to take care of any contingencies.

Then he sent a second telegram to Slim and Charlotte

Hanson.

Slim and Charlotte Hanson, Bandera, Texas

Sorry I had to leave so quickly. I would love to visit with you again

soon. If you come to Austin, I'll try to watch for you.

Aunt Mae

He felt Slim would know who sent it and be able to read between the lines. John didn't have to wait long. Within a week, he watched as Slim and Charlotte rode into town in their buggy. John had calculated the quickest they could get there and started sitting on Congress Avenue to wait. He watched them as they registered at the Depot Hotel and then followed them up to their room. After the porter departed, John knocked on the door. Charlotte answered, saw John and threw herself at him, wrapping him in her arms. John was surprised with how comfortable he felt hugging Charlotte, even in front of her father. After a lengthy hug, he released his grip but Charlotte was still holding on. Finally, she released him, backed up a step, and then leaned in and kissed him softly on the lips. John again embraced her without shame or modesty.

A few moments later, John became aware of Slim clearing his throat repeatedly. John was not sure how long he had been doing that, but realized he had completely forgotten about her father's presence.

"Well John, I must say it is good to see you. I wasn't sure if I would ever see you again. And I see that Charlotte's also happy to see you." Charlotte blushed slightly but then leaned in and kissed John again on the lips.

John didn't know what to make of his emotions. Charlotte was the only woman he had ever kissed. What he knew was that he liked it—a lot—even with her father present. He also had a very uneasy feeling in his stomach. He already had a feeling of the path his life was going to take and knew instinctively if anyone other than Slim knew of his feelings for Charlotte, she would be at risk, even more than Jesse had been. He shuddered at the thought of what had happened to the gentle giant of a man who once called him *Little Buddy*. The memory brought a smile to his face and a tear to his eye.

John vowed then he would never put Charlotte at risk. Whatever it took to keep her and Slim safe was worth it. He also realized in that moment, unless the direction of his life changed significantly, he could never again allow himself to become close to anyone. The solitude of his life gave him pause and sadness. But he knew his mission from here on out was to balance the Scales of Justice, whatever it took.

Immediately, John was conflicted. He didn't think he was above the law or that he was somehow so special he was the one chosen to dispense justice. What he did know was that someone had to bring justice when justice was denied to so many. He realized that he could not correct every injustice but he needed to carefully discern when justice was likely to be denied to a person and then determine how he was to intervene.

Ever since he first learned to defend himself in the boxing club at Georgetown Prep, John realized he could do what was necessary when called on. And he didn't have any pangs of conscience when he knew he was doing the right thing. He knew someone had to do it. For whatever reason, he felt he was the one equipped to do the job.

As he reflected on his life, he realized there were many things that made him perfect for this role. First, his stature. He was shorter than most men and many women. Most men didn't even notice him when he walked in a room or rode down the street. And those who did usually just thought how odd it was for such a little man to be riding such a big horse. He also knew he had an uncommon ability with his fists and he had absolutely no fear of facing an opponent of any size.

Finally, over the past eighteen months, he had gained such proficiency with his six-gun and knives that he knew he could hit any target with deadly results. John was singularly prepared for the mission before him. But he also reflected on his strict religious training and how he had a sense that God was always watching and cared deeply about all that happened in the world. John made up his mind he would never be arrogant with his defensive capabilities. He saw them as gifts given from on High to do what needed to be done. And he would never be so arrogant as to think he was doing God's work or that he was God's avenger. But he did feel he could correct significant injustices and still bow to his Creator.

Slim asked John to be seated in the parlor of their suite. He sat on the settee and Charlotte sat beside him, placing her hands in her lap in a prim and proper fashion. John wanted to put his arm around her or to at least take her hand. He stifled both urges for the sake of her father's presence.

"Well John, we obviously got your message, so we came as soon as possible. What on earth got you to leave town in such a rush?"

"Slim, I don't even know where to start. But I guess I

need to start with Jesse. I know he was killed because of a conversation he had with me at your ranch. Someone overheard us. Now I know it was Cody and Gus. They murdered him in the saloon and Betsy was part of it. I also found out the entire town council has been involved in wholesale murder when their extortion efforts were unsuccessful. Each of them, including Betsy and Sally, has murdered many times. They're stealin' the town blind and they don't care who gets in the way. They had Marshal Edwards murdered and used me to get rid of his murderer. And as far as I can determine there is nothin' anyone can do about it."

John continued, "As you know, Marshal Edwards was gonna contact the Texas Rangers and get them to come in and correct the wrongs in Bandera. He was murdered before that happened. But even if he had contacted them, nothing would have happened. The council is paying off someone high up in the state police and they also have a well-placed contact in the governor's office."

"I can't believe that," replied Slim. Charlotte let out a gasp and grabbed the neck of her dress. "How could they have that kind of power?"

"It's obvious to me they have been fleecing the town

for years. I think the judge is the ringleader but I'm also convinced that they're all equally guilty. Even if the judge or the mayor was to be gone, the corruption would continue.

"I'm not sure how to explain what I have on my mind except to give you a bit of history of my life." John looked at the floor, swallowed and then continued. "Ever since I was a youngster, I have had a heart for helping those who didn't have a voice and those who were denied justice. I thought my life would find meaning in being a lawyer. That is why I went to law school. I wanted to be the one who could help those who had no one to stand up for them. In law school, I found joy in studying the law and understanding how important it is for all people to have equal access to the law. I was introduced to the Scales of Justice. Each time I looked at that statue, I could feel the Scales of Justice in my mind. I was determined to do what I could to see that the scales were balanced.

"What you don't know about me is that my parents were very wealthy and after they passed away, they left me their fortune. I not only don't have any financial needs but I am in a position that I can provide financial help to those who need it. So far, there hasn't been as much of a need to help people financially as there has been to help them achieve justice.

"In looking for a place to practice law, I was drawn to Bandera. Even after I realized there was little need for an attorney there, I still felt Bandera was to be my home. Then, when the marshal was murdered and I was asked to take his place, I thought perhaps being a lawman was what I was destined to do. For the first few weeks, I was content. I saw the council as allies and enjoyed the long hours of protecting the citizens of Bandera."

Charlotte and Slim listened silently as John continued.

"It wasn't long until the council made it clear my main job was in serving them. I was to serve warrants, subpoenas, and other legal documents so the council could collect unjust debts. And the payoff for the marshal was that he was paid for every action where a paper was served. I was told that Marshal Edwards made an additional four thousand dollars a year serving papers. And Clem Williams made an extra two thousand dollars."

Slim's eyes showed his shock and disbelief. How could two individuals make such money in a small town like Bandera? And if they were making that much, how much more was the town council making? Slim and Charlotte realized John was right in the danger that he felt and about his need to leave town immediately.

"So what are you gonna do?" Slim asked.

"Well, one thing I know is I can't put you and Charlotte in danger. And if anyone knows we have any contact at all, your lives will be cut short. For that reason, I don't think we can allow anyone to ever see us in public or know we have any contact with each other."

"Ever?" asked Charlotte.

"At least for as far as I can see into the future. Admittedly, that is not very far right now. As long as one single member of the council or their contacts in Austin remains alive, the two of you are at risk. And the only way I remain safe is if I never again use the name John Crudder. As far as anyone else is concerned, I have gone back to New York City and will die there in obscurity."

"John, when I hired you to work at my ranch, I never dreamed I was putting your life at risk. I'm sorry I ever offered you a job."

"Don't be, Slim, someone needed to intervene in Bandera. I have a feelin' I am here for a purpose. And I'm not gonna slink from my responsibilities. Regardless of the personal cost, I have a job to do."

"I agree, John," said Slim.

"I'm so proud of you, John," said Charlotte. With those words, John got a tear in his eye.

"I'm sorry. Did I say something wrong?"

"No. It's just that I had always wanted to hear my father say that," said John. "Just before his death, my father sent me a telegram telling me he was proud of me. And then at my father's funeral, his long-time business manager told me the same thing. I never realized how affirming those words can be."

"John, I *am* proud of you," Charlotte repeated.

"And so am I," added Slim.

John let the words sink in as he looked at the floor. Then he raised his head and got back to business.

"I'm not sure how or when it will happen, but I have to balance the Scales of Justice in Bandera. I'm sure I will need your help but right now, I don't know what help that might be. We must be careful. When we communicate, I will always be Aunt Mae. And we must use the most circumspect language. Be very careful, don't ever mention my name or become part of any conversation about me. The more you can move me to the distant past in your memory, the better."

"I agree," Slim replied. "From now on, it will be as if

you had never been to Bandera."

"And Charlotte, as much as I don't like the idea, you need to go out with other men. I don't want to take the risk anyone will think you are saving yourself for me."

"But I am, John. I hope you know that by now."

"I reckon I did. I'm glad to hear you say it anyway. But Charlotte, that may be a long wait. I will not do anything that will ever put you at risk. The best thing you can do is to put me out of your mind."

"Well forget that, John. I'll never put you out of my mind. I can act the part and even go out with other men but will never put you out of my mind. You're part of me and always will be."

With that John put his arms around her and she rested her head on his shoulder. She wept bitter tears for she knew it might be a long time before she felt his arms around her again. After several minutes, John pulled away.

"I better get going. And the first thing in the morning, you better get going as well. Remember, none of us know who the council's confederates are in Austin. Every person you meet should be seen as a potential enemy. Be very careful in what you say and who you talk to."

And with that, John was gone. Within the next few

minutes, John had checked out of the hotel and walked down to the livery stable to get Midnight. He stroked the great stallion, and whispered in his ear for which he got a nice whinny and a shake of the stallion's head.

John saddled up and headed north. *It's time for me to get out of this county. I must become a cipher. The easiest way to do that is to go to a raucous city and become a really little man there. Fort Worth is where I need to go.*

Midnight acted like he could read John's mind and started into a gentle lope. John whistled as he rode the trail toward Fort Worth. He knew there were going to be some difficult days ahead. But he also knew he was now very clear on the direction of his life. With that clarity, he set his mind and rode north.

CHAPTER 17: 1871

John made his way to Fort Worth and arrived after ten days, riding no more than thirty miles a day. He knew Midnight could easily do twice that because of the horse's incredible endurance and his light weight. But he was in no hurry. He had a lot of things to think about.

He tied Midnight to the hitching rail in front of one of the saloons, ducked under the rail, and went to the front door. John figured there were more saloons in Fort Worth than there were just a year ago. He thought there were too many saloons then and he felt the town was surely suffering because of them.

John was in a part of Forth Worth known as *Hell's Half*

Acre. There were many such places in the west but none as rowdy as in this city. The streets were dotted with bawdy houses, saloons, and flop houses that were used by the trail riders who wanted to sleep in a bed instead of on the ground for a night.

Walking to the swinging doors of the saloon, John realized he was not tall enough to see over the short doors but had to push through them before he could see inside. As was often the case, he heard a cowboy chuckle seeing such a short man enter the saloon. Mercifully, John was spared any comment about his short stature. His hide was tough but still he wanted to just blend in and not be the focus of attention. Within seconds of entering the bar, the other patrons went back to their own conversations and ignored the petite cowboy.

John walked to the end of the bar and was going to order a beer, when he realized the bar was so tall that it came about chin high. Instead, he chose a chair at a table in the corner. A waitress anticipated his order and brought him a beer.

"Will there be anything else, honey?" asked the waitress.

"No thanks," replied John, as he placed a quarter on the table and said, "The rest is yours if you will just answer a few questions for me."

"Just name it honey."

"First I need a room in town that doesn't cost much. Where would you suggest?"

"There is the hotel, of course. But if you want good food and cheap rent, I would recommend the boardin' house next to the livery. You can't miss it. So what's your other question, honey?" she asked as she batted her eyelashes.

"I was thinkin' I needed some work for a few weeks," said John. "Any ideas who might be hiring?"

"Hon, this is Fort Worth. Not many people hiring," said the waitress. "But there's work to be had if you can find it."

"It looks like there are hands a'plenty here," said John.

"These are trail hands. There's a different bunch here every day. They come into town with a trail ride. They get their pay and either drink it up, gamble it away, or give it to some floosy in one of the other saloons. Bear in mind, they won't find anyone like that here," she said with eyes flashing and her hand on her hip.

John nodded his thanks and took a big swallow of his beer.

"Well hon, if you want to ask any more questions be

sure to come back in later on. I get off at six in case you're interested."

John smiled weakly and took another swallow of beer. What he wanted more than anything was to get out of there and never come back. Before he could leave, a barroom tussle broke out around him. It quickly escalated so John picked up his beer and moved further into the corner of the bar. The brawl ended with a professional gambler pulling a gun on someone who looked like a local farmer or rancher. The poor man didn't stand a chance against someone who was only interested in gaining as much money as he could.

As John watched, the gambler shot the poor farmer twice. And after he hit the floor, the gambler stood over him and put another bullet into the man's chest. John recalled that was the same thing he had seen Harvey Fowler do in his bank in Bandera. He was appalled by what he witnessed. John also realized he was stunned with the lack of emotion of the gambler.

A deputy marshal ran through the swinging doors with his gun out. "What happened here?"

"He tried to cheat me at cards and then tried to pull a gun on me. I had no choice but to shoot him. The bartender will back me up."

The deputy put his gun away and said, "Then clean this mess up. It seems the same thing happens in here every week. You sure get more than your share of bad customers."

Just as in Bandera, it appeared the gambler would get away with murder. And it didn't appear this was his first. John held his place but he wondered what it would have felt like to draw down on the gambler. There was not a doubt he could take the gunman.

John walked out and took the reins from the hitching rail, mounted Midnight, and turned toward the livery stable he spotted when he entered town. There he unsaddled Midnight, groomed him and paid for a week's worth of oats and stall rental. Truth be known, he would be just as happy to bed down in the stall with Midnight.

But he walked next door and got a room for a week. He told the clerk he would return later and fill out the register properly. John was not sure how long he would stay but he felt sure it would be a least a week. Then he walked down to the telegraph office and sent Slim and Charlotte another message:

Slim and Charlotte Hanson, Bandera, Texas

Arrived in Fort Worth. Nice town. Will stay here for a while and take in the culture. Write when you have time.

Aunt Mae

The telegraph operator looked at him quizzically. John said, "My aunt is in poor health so I'm sending a message for her. If there is ever a reply, just keep the message here. I'll check in every few days." With that the operator took John's payment and turned and sent the message while John waited. He also presented identification and collected the money Mr. Hastings sent.

Leaving the telegraph office, John walked down the long broad Main Street. After a bit, he came upon a haberdashery at the corner of Main and Second Street that had a *Help Wanted* sign in the window. On a whim, John removed his hat and walked in. He visited with the proprietor and then inquired about the job. Looking at John, the shop owner shook his head.

"I think you would do well in a feed store or workin' at the livery stable," the owner said. "No offense meant. But here, we sell quality men's wear. We have the finest suits from Philadelphia. I don't mean to offend you sir, but I need someone who understands fashion and can relate to my sophisticated clientele."

"I can understand your concern and no offense taken. When I moved from New York, I gradually left behind my tailor-made suits. In Denver, I even traded my custom boots for this well-worn pair so I could fit in a bit better in the west. And I think I could relate to your customers. I received two degrees from Harvard and one from Oxford."

The haberdasher stood with his mouth half opened and speechless. After a moment he stuttered, "Well, sir, I, I, I, don't quite know what to say. Certainly, your speech belies your clothing. If you could come up with a presentable wardrobe, I would be pleased to have you in my employment."

"That sounds fine to me," replied John. Then he realized he needed to introduce himself. He should have thought about this before coming in the store. His thoughts went back to the gravestones near his father's grave: Alexander Hamilton and Robert Fulton. "My name is Hamilton. Robert Hamilton. You may call me Robert." John thought Robert would be easy to remember and to respond to since it was also his father's name.

"Well, Mr. Hamilton. Robert. My name is Mr. Asbury." The shop owner extended his hand. John shook it and Mr. Asbury added, "You're sure you have an appropriate wardrobe?"

"Not at the present. But I intend to be a good customer

before this day is over."

"Now sir, I am not in the practice of extending credit to an employee. Especially one who has not yet gone to work for me."

"And I wouldn't think of asking for credit. I can pay for what I purchase. I would like to start with five suits, ten shirts, appropriate under garments, a top coat, a derby hat, a cane, preferably with ivory inlays. Also, have me fitted for a nice pair of black boots. Oh, yes, and I will require several ties and silk handkerchiefs in assorted colors."

"And you actually have money to pay for all of that?"

John was enjoying himself as he reached into his pocket and revealed a thick stack of folded bills. Mr. Asbury looked at the size of John's bankroll and actually clicked his heels and said, "Certainly Sir. I will get started immediately gathering my best suits for you to inspect."

After making his clothing selections, John asked Mr. Asbury to measure his frame and then make sure the suits and shirts conformed to his build. "I would rather not try them on until I get a bath. I'm sure with your experience you will have no problem in getting my size correct."

"Yes, sir, I will be able to make all adjustments that are needed. I can't promise they will fit as well as custom-tailored suits but I do believe you will be very happy with the outcome. And I will work through the evening and have them all ready by morning."

"That's not necessary," John sighed. "Typically, I would ask you to have the clothes sent up to my room at the boarding house, but in this case, if you would be kind enough to hem up one pair of trousers, I have a bit of business to attend to and I'll come back here to collect that change of clothes. Then tomorrow, I can make the delivery of anything you have altered for me as my first order of business as your new employee. Would that be all right with you?"

"Absolutely. Absolutely, Mr. Hamilton," answered the store owner.

"And when I come back," John said, "I will no longer be Mr. Hamilton but just Robert."

"Very good, Mr. Hamilton. You will go from being my number one customer to being my number one employee.

"We haven't talked about your salary. I'm afraid I am not going to be able to pay you what you are accustomed to earning or certainly not what you will be worth to me in sales that I know you will make," Mr. Asbury lamented.

"I assume you're gonna pay me the customary wage and

that it will be fair. Is that true, Mr. Asbury?"

"Indeed it is, Mr. Hamilton. Indeed, it is."

"That is fine, Mr. Asbury. I trust you." And with that John put his fingers to his forehead as though he were tipping his hat, turned, and walked out the door. John thought it was great fun to purchase a new wardrobe. And he thought it would be enjoyable working as a clothing salesman. After all, he did need a totally new identity as he contemplated his next move.

On the walk back to the boarding house, John's jolly attitude soon left as he was again reminded of the badly out-of-balance Scales of Justice. He came there with the injustice in Bandera being his overwhelming thought but realized there was a more immediate need for justice in Fort Worth.

John thought about the gambler and knew he would soon set things right with him. And regardless of how long it took, John was committed to bringing justice back to Bandera. He knew the only way that would happen would be for him to take total responsibility for making it happen.

CHAPTER 18: 1871

John went to the bank and opened an account with the money Mr. Hastings sent, then went to pick up his new suit of clothes. After properly registering and taking his new clothes to his room, John got to thinking about the gambler he watched commit murder. John slipped back into the saloon in time to see the gambler walk up the stairs behind the bar. He realized the gambler made his home in the saloon, even if it was just for the time since he had drifted into Fort Worth.

Crudder walked out of the saloon and around back and found another staircase. He climbed the stairs and looked through the small window in the door at the top of the stairs. The gambler was exiting his room and returning to the saloon. John quietly stepped back down the stairs and contemplated his next move.

Crudder hurried back to the saloon where he got a beer and had a seat in the back corner. The gambler returned and took up his place at the table where he had left his deck of cards. Cowboys were just beginning to drift in for an evening of drinking and lewd talk with the two waitresses.

The gambler shuffled the deck over and over again as he carefully appraised each person who entered. John thought he had the look of a mountain lion sizing up his prey. John wasn't sure what he was looking for in a likely target but he continued to watch the gambler assessing each man.

Just after dusk, a group of cowboys came in laughing and carrying on with each other. It was evident that they were friends—probably just finishing a trail drive together. John also suspected that they had started drinking before they got to town. His hunch was verified when he heard one of the cowboys shout with a slur, "Barkeep! Set up me and my friends with a beer. And here's two silver dollars. One for the beer and one for you. We just got paid and we plan to drink up most of it t'night."

John saw the gambler's eyes narrow as he focused on

his prey. After the cowboys had half finished their beers, the gambler called out to them.

"You boys want to play some cards?" The cowboys looked at each other and laughed.

"You don't know what you're askin' mister. We're pretty good. We play poker might near every night on the trail. You sure you want to tangle with us?"

"Poker you say," said the gambler. "I'm not too good at poker but I'll risk it if you want to play a few hands."

The cowboys laughed again and all four sat down at the table with the professional gambler. The gambler set the cards in the middle of the table and suggested they cut them to see who would shuffle. One of the cowboys won the deal as a barmaid refilled their glasses. The cards were dealt and bets placed. After three rounds of bets and raises, the gambler threw in his cards and the game continued. The pot grew to more than ten dollars. Then on the final hand, one of the cowboys threw down three queens, winning the pot.

The gambler shook his head in mock exasperation. The cards were dealt again. The pot grew to more than thirty dollars as the cowboys recklessly gambled away several weeks of hard earned pay. The gambler stayed with them through three more rounds. He had contributed about five dollars to the pot then threw in his cards as he announced that it just wasn't his night.

John watched from the shadows as the gambler skillfully egged on the cowboys, encouraging them to bet more and more. They bet recklessly and raised and folded until each of them had won at least one pot. With the exception of the contribution the gambler made to each pot, John estimated that the cowboys were coming out about even. They kept playing and consuming their fourth beer as the barmaid came by with another round.

Then as John had expected, the gambler took his turn at dealing. The betting continued to grow with each round. Finally, they were betting everything in their pockets.

John watched the gambler deal and even from several yards away, he could tell he was dealing from the bottom of the deck. He then watched as the gambler pulled a card from his sleeve on the last hand. Skillfully, he palmed one of the cards, folded it with one hand, and slipped it into his vest pocket.

Each player laid down his hand and the gambler's flush beat the rest. The moment he reached for the pot, one of the cowboys shouted, "Cheater!" and groggily stood up telegraphing that he was going to reach for his six-gun. The completely sober gambler easily pulled his own gun and shot the staggering cowboy before he even got his hand on his gun. One of his drunk friends went for his gun and met the same fate. The gambler stood up and said, "Either of you two boys want to join your friends?" One of the other cowboys lifted his hand and shook a finger at the gambler. The gambler quickly dispatched him too.

Within a few minutes, the same deputy John had seen earlier entered the saloon with his gun drawn and shouted, "What's goin' on here?"

The gambler calmly holstered his gun, sat down and answered, "Deputy, it seems these cowboys got drunk and decided they wanted to start shootin' people. I simply put an end to it."

"Anybody else see what happened?" asked the deputy.

"It's just as he said," replied the bartender. "They drew their guns and this man shot 'em in self-defense."

"Well clean this place up," yelled the deputy, "And don't have no more shootin' here tonight."

As the deputy left the saloon, the gambler raked in his winnings. The one remaining card-playing cowboy dragged his friends out of the saloon one at a time. When the floor was cleared, someone started playing the piano and the bartender shouted, "One round on the house for everyone."

Cheers went up from the gathered patrons and a festive atmosphere returned. The gambler returned to his card shuffling and waited for his next prey to approach his table. He didn't have to wait long for eager customers to lay their money down.

For John, the Scales of Justice that had already been tilted went wildly out of balance. He knew he had to do something. He couldn't stand the thought that the gambler might move on before paying for his crimes. *Tonight is as good of a night as any*, thought John. He went to the boarding house and to his room. There he picked up a short-handled shovel he bought earlier at the mercantile.

John Crudder figured the saloon was open until midnight or later and that the gambler would not likely leave until the last customer was gone. Just before midnight, John departed his room and went to the front of the saloon. He looked at the row of horses wondering which one belonged to the gambler. John smiled as he spotted an English saddle.

He untied the horse and moved it to the back of the saloon. John then went to the livery stable to saddle Midnight. There was no one there, which suited John just fine. He led Midnight down the street, placed the small shovel in his saddlebag, tied the stallion beside the gambler's horse, and silently climbed the stairs. John crept down the hall, entered the unlocked door of the gambler's room and waited with the lamp off.

In the early morning, the gambler came back to his room. As he lit the lamp, John silently waited to be noticed. When the gambler turned, he was startled to see John sitting in his room. "You're mighty fast with that gun. You don't give a man much of a chance."

"What business is it of yours, little man?" asked the gambler.

"I don't like to see people taken advantage of. Those cowboys were so drunk they were not a threat to you. In fact, one of them wasn't even wearin' a gun and none of them came close to hurting you."

"Why you snot-nosed little runt. I'm gonna teach you a thing or two." With that, the gambler drew his six-gun as he turned squarely to take aim at John. John had already drawn both daggers from the scabbards on his back and let them fly at the same time. Both found their mark deep in the neck of the gambler. There was a gurgling noise from the gambler as he stared in disbelief at John, grabbing his neck and silently dropping to the floor.

John moved in quickly and tied a bed sheet around the gambler's neck to staunch the flow of blood, cleaned his knives, and replaced them in their scabbards. He checked the hallway and satisfied himself there was no one around. Then he dragged the gambler down the back stairs. Leaving the body beneath the stairs for a few moments, John went to the hitching rail where he had left Midnight and the gambler's horse. He hoisted the body up onto the saddle and tied his hands and feet together beneath the horse.

Silently moving the horses to the shadows, John mounted Midnight and slipped out of town on a little used trail that didn't intersect any of the streets. He came to a meadow that was on the edge of a wash. At first he thought he would bury the gambler in the wash but realized the grave could be easily unearthed if there was a flood. Instead, he opted to dig in the soft earth of the meadow. It only took him a little while to get the grave a full six feet deep.

John untied the body and rolled it into the grave. After refilling the grave, John put down his shovel, removed his hat, and looked toward the sky.

"Lord, I'm not sure if this man had any redeeming qualities at all. But if he did, I hope you will remember them more than you remember the wretched way he murdered that farmer earlier today." He then slapped the gambler's horse across the rump, knowing by morning the animal would find its way back to town. John speculated that people would not miss the gambler and would assume he had just been thrown or that he left town in a hurry to escape someone he had cheated.

John transplanted tufts of prairie grass on the grave knowing that in a few days there would not be any evidence left of the digging. Picking up a nearby tree limb, John carefully removed the tracks of both horses and turned Midnight toward town. After a few minutes of grooming Midnight, John returned to the boarding house, drew a bath, shaved, and went to sleep.

Chapter 19: 1871

J ohn realized he had slept soundly throughout the night. Not only had his conscience not bothered him as he dispensed justice to the gambler, but he couldn't remember when he had slept better. The new course of his life had been set. But he also knew he would have to be very careful and only dispense his brand of justice on the worst of the worst.

John thoroughly enjoyed getting dressed in his new clothes and boots. They weren't nearly as expensive as what he had grown accustomed to in New York but they were still fine clothes. Donning his derby hat and picking up his cane, John walked slowly but confidently to his new place of employment.

Mr. Asbury was just unlocking the door when John arrived. "Well, Robert. I must say you do look handsome in your new clothes. Quite unlike the rough-looking cowboy who came in here yesterday." John accepted the compliment and reminded himself that he had to completely assume the identity of Robert Hamilton.

John took care of the first two customers who entered so Mr. Asbury could evaluate his sale's technique. The first customer was looking for a new shirt. John sold him two shirts, a suit, and several accessories. The second customer was just asking for directions but John sold him an umbrella and a pair of shoes.

"You must have sold a lot of clothes in the past," Mr. Asbury said, beaming at the quick sales John had made.

"Not really," replied John. "I just know what I like and want to try to help others find clothes they like."

"If you keep selling like that, I'm going to have to get some new stock in a hurry. In fact, I need to place an order today anyway. Your purchases yesterday left several empty places on my racks and shelves. You know, Robert, in all of the years I've been in business, I have never sold one customer as many clothes as I sold you yesterday. By the way, I'll make the alterations on the rest of your suits and shirts today if you can handle sales. And I must say that you handle sales much better than I."

"I'm glad to do so, Mr. Asbury. You can leave everything to me. If I have questions, I'll come to the back and ask."

The rest of the week, John handled all of the sales work while Mr. Asbury busied himself in the storeroom and occupied himself outside of the store. That suited John just fine. He liked working alone and found he had a knack for selling clothing. When the week ended, Mr. Asbury gleefully announced that they had just completed the best week of sales in the history of his store.

The next week, while Mr. Asbury was out about town, as had become his custom since John started working for him, John listened as two customers tried on boots and talked with each other about the disappearance of the gambler.

"I heard that he was caught cheating and he had to leave the city in a hurry," said one of the men.

The other said, "No, what happened was he was finally caught with the saloon owner's wife and took the late stage out of town." Both men laughed and then changed the subject.

John felt that he would not have to worry about anyone missing the gambler. Evidently, he was not well liked and probably had deserved worse than what he got from John. He reminded himself the actions that he take must be only for people who are beyond the reach of the law. In those cases, John felt justified in balancing the scales.

In the afternoon, Mr. Asbury came back in the shop and told John he could take a break to get something to eat. John walked down to the telegraph office to see if he had a response from Slim and Charlotte. He was delighted to find that he did have a message. It read:

Aunt Mae, Fort Worth, Texas

Good to hear from you. Have lots of interesting information to give you at your next visit. Probably not best to come back for three or four months. Seems you have been missed.

Slim and Charlotte

John read the telegram and then sat down and composed a response. He knew from their message that there were some complications but was not sure what. But he was also patient. He knew he could wait as long as was necessary to right the many wrongs he had seen in Bandera.

Slim and Charlotte Hanson, Bandera, Texas

Will plan on visiting after Christmas. Anxious to see you and hear your news. Let me know if things change.

Aunt Mae

It was time for John to be patient. He knew he couldn't risk going back to Bandera for at least six months. By Christmas, he felt he could start moving south again and balance the scales. Meanwhile, he settled into his new life as a store clerk.

John enjoyed his new routine as Robert Hamilton, seller of fine men's clothes. He worked all day selling clothes and then in the evening he would go to the boarding house. John seldom had conversations with anyone outside of the store. With customers, he adopted a bit of the snooty British attitude and even a bit of a British accent the Savile Row clerks had when he bought clothes there. He found the customers regarded his demeanor as sophisticated but that also meant there was no idle chitchat with them and no personal information exchanged. This suited John just fine for he was able to remain virtually anonymous in the city.

Mr. Asbury told John thanks to him, the store had just completed the most successful month in the store's history. He also told him the British accent was helping his sales. John determined then that he would become as thoroughly British as possible. And with Mr. Asbury's encouragement, his British accent became even stronger.

"Robert," Mr. Asbury continued, "I don't know how I ever managed without you. You have indeed earned your keep. As a reward, beginning next month, I'm going to increase your salary by one dollar a week. During the course of a year, you should be able to save a significant amount of money."

"Thank you, Mr. Asbury," John replied and bowed deeply. "I certainly do appreciate that. And you're right. I should be able to save some money by the end of the year." Little did Asbury know that John's wealth was probably greater than the combined total of every person in the city. Certainly, the salary was not important to John. What was important was he was able to have time to contemplate his future as a vigilante. That was a word John found hard to use about himself but he knew it was an accurate description of what e had committed himself to do.

He thought about how quietly and efficiently he had eliminated the gambler. John considered himself as a deliverer of justice—a person who worked alone and in the dark. He wondered if perhaps he should adopt a moniker that suited his alter identity?

Maybe he should think of himself as the Twilight

Deliverer. The name suited him. But he also realized that he would likely never speak that name aloud.

The sad thing for John was recognizing that the new path of his life meant he would likely have to live alone for the rest of his days. If he tried to have a family, he knew he would make them targets if his identity were discovered. That was a sacrifice he was willing to make. He reasoned that someone had to look out for those who would not get justice otherwise.

CHAPTER 20: 1872

A couple of weeks after Christmas, John decided it was time to head back to Bandera. He had previously given Mr. Asbury a four-week notice of his departure. Asbury understandably was reluctant to lose his ace salesman. He did all he could to talk John out of his departure.

"Mr. Asbury, I don't mean to be presumptuous, but if you would like, I can teach you some of the things I learned both in London on Savile Row and in the New York Garment District." Mr. Asbury's eyes grew bigger and he eagerly agreed that he would love to be a student under "Robert's" tutelage.

"Robert, you tell me what to do and how you are so successful in sales and I will do my best to be a good pupil."

"I have one condition, Mr. Asbury. The condition is that you not discuss me or my past and not engage in conversation about me when I'm gone. The reason is that I enjoy living in virtual anonymity, which I have enjoyed my entire time in Fort Worth."

"I'm not sure I understand but you can count on me, Robert," responded Asbury. "And if your name comes up in conversation, I'll simply say my salesman had to go back to London."

"That will be fine, Mr. Asbury. Besides, I am keeping a room at the boarding house and intend to return to Fort Worth from time to time. I might even want to see you about employment once again."

"Robert, you can have a job any time you want it. Even if I had ten men working for me, I know you would be able to make sales no one else could."

"All right then. Let's start school." John and Mr. Asbury walked back to the rows of suits. The section for fine men's clothes was several times larger now than it was when John first arrived. It was John's responsibility to order what was necessary for the store.

First John walked from suit to suit and told Asbury things about the suits the storeowner never knew. "This one is made of worsted wool. While there are not many men wearing wool suits here now, I believe you will find that you can sell a lot of these in the fall and winter. They wear well and hold their shape nicely. Then for those who have realized the extra warmth offered by a winter wool suit, they will naturally want something in silk or linen for the spring and summer."

John talked to him about each suit's style and cut. He showed Asbury code on the tags that indicated some of the suits were cut slim and others had a fuller cut. Asbury said, "I never knew that. Before you got here, I only carried one line of suits and they were all cut the same. The only difference was that some of them were larger and some were smaller."

After giving Asbury a thorough education in fine men's clothing, he went on to talk about custom tailoring. Asbury was a willing and able student. John showed him some additional but simple alterations he could make that would make an off-the-rack suit close to a custom suit.

"But Mr. Asbury, if you really want to set your store apart from others, you should consider giving customers the opportunity to order bespoke suits from you," John added in a matter-of-fact manner.

"Robert, I don't know anything about making a custom-tailored suit. I'm pretty good making alterations and I'm very precise when I measure but that is the extent of my skills with a sewing machine."

"There is a way to add a custom line of suits for those discriminating customers who demand quality. I have discovered that several of the men I have sold suits to often travel to Dallas to get suits custom tailored since they are not available in Fort Worth."

"I know that's true, and I even thought about offering Mr. Wong at the laundry the opportunity to make some suits for me. I know he worked for a tailor when he was in China."

"I was not aware of that. And that may be a good idea. However, if he becomes the custom suit maker in town, you may just end up making him a successful competitor."

"I certainly don't want to do that. I have enough competition in town as it is. So, what do you have in mind?"

"I would be glad to contact my suit makers in both London and New York and see if they would make suits for you according to the measurements you supply. I think they would be able to provide you with a completed suit that is close to the same price you are paying now for factory-made suits from Philadelphia. Then when the suit comes in, you make the final adjustments for each customer. That way they get a tailor-made suit that comes out of New York or London that is further tailored by you. I can show you the additional measurements you will need to order custom-made suits."

John spent the rest of the afternoon showing Asbury how to make measurements when making a suit from scratch. He then went over to the telegraph office and sent telegrams to both of his suit makers. In less than two days, both tailors had responded favorably to John's proposal. Asbury had a sign painted that proclaimed the addition of custom-tailored suits from both London and New York. Customer response was almost immediate. Asbury was surprised so many men in Fort Worth were interested in tailor-made suits.

For the next few weeks, Asbury first watched John measure and take orders for suits. Then he helped John. Then Asbury was taking orders for suits like he had been doing it for his entire career.

Before John left Fort Worth, the first suits ordered

from New York had arrived along with several books of cloth swatches. Asbury was in his element making the final measurements on his customers, just as he had done for years with the factory-made suits. John made a similar contact for shirt makers in both fashion capitals and Asbury hurried off to the sign maker to get yet another sign for his ever-expanding line of custom apparel.

John decided it was time for him to get himself a nice wardrobe so on his last day at work he said, "I think I'm going to need some new clothes because I need to leave Fort Worth. Mr. Asbury, do I have your permission to take off work early today and become a customer?"

Asbury smiled, remembering the first time John had become his customer. "Absolutely, Robert. I mean, Mr. Hamilton. In what would you be interested?"

John got out the cloth swatches that had just come in from London a couple of weeks before and selected several in lightweight wool and several in silk. He even ordered a couple of seersucker suits. In all, he ordered twelve suits and twenty shirts.

"Mr. Hamilton," Asbury beamed as he offered his hand to John. "You're the best customer ever. And Robert, you're the best salesman I've ever met. The next time you're back in town, I will do a final fitting on your new wardrobe."

John shook his hand and then went to the boarding house and settled his bill. He paid for his room for the next year, and asked the owner to simply watch out for his things while he was gone. The owner agreed and John went down to the livery stable, saddled Midnight, and headed south.

CHAPTER 21: 1872

John Crudder was traveling light. The first thing he had packed in his saddlebag was his short-handled shovel. He had a feeling he was going to need it in Bandera. He also packed flour, bacon, coffee, and a bit of sugar. One last thing he added to his saddlebags was a pint of whiskey. Although he never drank anything but beer, he knew it might come in handy if he needed to clean a wound.

Midnight moved into a gentle lope, as John left town. It wasn't long before the great horse broke into a run. John laughed aloud as he realized again how much his stallion loved to run. After about fifteen minutes, he slowed Midnight down to a walk. John was determined to take his time getting to Bandera. He figured if he covered about fifteen miles a day he would be to Bandera in less than three weeks. That suited John fine for he relished having the time to think. Saddle time was John's best thinking time.

While the pace was appropriate for John, Midnight was anxious to get on with the journey. Each day over the next three weeks, John would find an open stretch of prairie and give Midnight his head. Each time the stallion ran at full speed, John laughed with glee. He wasn't sure which of them was having the most fun.

About two day's ride from Bandera, John began skirting the town to the west. He knew he would have to contend with more hills in that direction but he also reasoned that he would be less likely to run into any other riders. John went on south of Bandera almost to Hondo. He then cut across the H&F and headed back north to the ranch headquarters.

Arriving about suppertime, John wished he could ride up to the dining hall and join the other hands he had learned to respect and value. But he knew to do so would only put them at risk. And it would put Slim and Charlotte at even greater risk.

While the hands all gathered in the dining hall, John quickly penned a note to Charlotte.

Bring your Dad. Our special place on the Medina River. Midnight.

He slipped up to Charlotte's window that stood open, reached inside and placed the note on the table under the lamp. He knew she would see the note when she lit the lamp after supper. And he was sure she had not forgotten the picnic they shared beside the river one Sunday afternoon the year before.

Shortly after midnight, John spotted the buggy in the moonlight coming down the trail. As it pulled to a stop near the river, John called softly, "Please don't make any noise. I don't want to put either of you at risk."

Charlotte let out a gasp and looked like she was going to call out to John. Her father quickly put his hand to her mouth. She shook her head that she understood.

John walked to the side of the buggy and helped Charlotte down. She threw her arms around him and hugged him without making a sound. Slim gave up waiting for them to move and climbed out the other side of the buggy.

Charlotte finally released John and he offered his hand to Slim. Slim shook it and slapped him on the back. "John, it's good to see you again."

"I missed you so," said Charlotte. "I want you here with

me."

John smiled and nodded his head. "I would like that too but I can't take a chance on you getting hurt because of me."

Charlotte seemed to accept his explanation but pouted to show that she didn't have to like it. John put his arm around her for comfort. He surprised himself he would do that in front of her father but he knew Slim trusted and respected him.

"We didn't know where you're goin' from here, so we packed you some provisions."

"Thanks, Slim. Now let's get down to business. You said you have news and not to come back too soon. What'd you find out?"

Slim started, "You're right in ridin' out when you did. And you're right that they murdered Jesse because they thought he told you somethin' about their operation. We're just not sure what they thought Jesse told you."

"What Jesse told me," John continued, "is that he found the rest of the rustlers over on the ranch near Tarpley that sold a couple of years ago. He said he heard them talking about stealing cattle from all of the ranches around here. But he got spooked then and slipped away before he could hear anything more.

"When Jesse was tellin' me, I saw someone slip into the shadows behind the barn. It must have been Cody and Gus 'cause they're the ones who took him to town and then murdered him."

"The important thing," Slim exclaimed, "is that we're sure the judge is the ring leader of all that is goin' on in Bandera. We have watched the interactions of the town council with him and it is obvious he is the one who directs all that takes place here. And that's in keepin' with what you've found, John. The meetings are always in his office and he always presides."

"Well, Slim, I think it's time we kill a snake."

"What do you mean?" asked Charlotte.

"How do you kill a snake?" John asked rhetorically. "You cut off its head."

Slim nodded in agreement. Charlotte shuddered as she considered the meaning of John's words. John stood without emotion for he had already made peace with what needed to be done.

"That probably won't solve the problem but it's the place to start. I don't want you involved in this at all. I'll do what needs to be done and then get out of town. In a little while, I'll contact you. Together, we'll figure out the next steps."

Slim nodded in agreement. Charlotte threw her arms around John again.

"I don't want to lose you," Charlotte cried. "I don't know what I would do if anything happened to you."

"Don't worry about me. I can take care of myself and I don't take chances. When the time is right, I'll do what needs to be done."

With those words, John turned, mounted Midnight, and rode toward Austin. He didn't want to take a chance that anyone had seen him around Bandera. John couldn't take a chance of putting Slim and Charlotte at risk.

CHAPTER 22: 1872

O ver the next several weeks, John Crudder became more settled into his role as the Twilight Deliverer. The course of his life had been set. There was no turning back.

Bandera was a nice town that harbored a cesspool of corruption, greed, and murder. John knew his work was crucial to the town's survival. Without his intervention, he felt the town would eventually dry up and become just another ghost town. He was determined not to let that happen.

It was time to leave Austin and go back to Bandera. John saddled Midnight and set his course for the southwest.

He was in no hurry. He planned on taking a week to get there, though he knew he could do it in half that time on Midnight.

As he rode, he was careful to watch for other riders. When he saw any sign of others on the trail, John moved out several miles so he could parallel the trail without being seen. Each day, John's resolve to balance the Scales of Justice solidified.

On his eighth day out of Austin, he made camp about five miles outside of Bandera. John selected a spot where he had previously camped. He knew Midnight could easily find the way to town later, even on such a moonless night.

Judging from the stars, John felt it was the middle of the night. Time for him to ride! He broke camp, erased any sign of his presence, and walked Midnight toward town.

At the edge of town, John tied Midnight and continued on foot the rest of the way. He walked up the alley behind the judge's house, pausing often to make sure there was no movement or sign of any other person.

As he stepped around the corner of the mercantile, he stepped on a cat that let out a loud cry. John froze and moved back into the shadow. After about five minutes, he was convinced the cat didn't disturb anyone. He crouched and gently moved each foot forward, carefully placing each boot down on its side and keeping his heels off the ground. He continued his silent journey until he got to the judge's house.

John knew the judge slept upstairs in the back corner of the house. He also knew to get to the judge, he had to get past Cora Potter, the judge's housekeeper. Her room was just inside the back door.

Crudder slipped around behind the judge's house. He placed a slim knife between the door and doorframe, flipping the latch out of the way. Cora Potter's bedroom was just inside the door across the hall from the kitchen. John could hear her rhythmic breathing as he made his way past her half-opened door to the base of the stairs. He climbed to the top of the stairs and paused to listen.

John paused outside the door to the bedroom and listened to Judge Gideon's loud snoring. Slipping a candle from his pocket, Crudder lit it and cupped his hand around the flame to contain the light. Looking away from the flame to preserve his ability to see in the dark, John allowed the candle to burn until it was dripping down all sides. He blew out the flame and quietly turned the knob of the judge's bedroom. Carefully closing the door behind him, John stood in the shadows and allowed his eyes to adjust to the darkness.

Silently, John reached his left hand up his sleeve and removed the dagger from its scabbard. He approached the judge's bed and listened to the contented snoring coming from the man who had so callously cheated and robbed the citizens of Bandera, all of the time being revered as a pillar of the community.

John placed the warm candle on the judge's nightstand, clamped his right hand over the judge's mouth and then instantly placed the end of the dagger into the edge of the judge's ear.

"If you value the life of Cora Potter, you'll not make a sound or move at all. If you do, I will be forced to take her life as well. Tonight is judgment day for you. I am your judge and I will be your executioner. I am gonna remove my hand from your mouth but if you make a sound, you are deciding to end Ms. Potter's life. Do you understand?"

The judge nodded. Crudder said, "Judge, do you recognize my voice?"

The judge nodded.

"Judge Gideon Anderson, you have been found guilty of murder, theft, and numerous other crimes as you have lined your pockets and those of the other five members of the town council. You have been sentenced to death. Judge, you used your position and influence to enrich yourself and the other five council members. Your guilt is greater than theirs. My only regret is that I can only execute you once for your crimes. Do you have anything to say before I carry out your sentence?"

Judge Anderson, began to weep, and meekly said, "Who do you think you are taking justice into your own hands? Are you some kind of midnight marauder?"

The judge's weeping got louder. "I never meant to hurt anybody. And I only wanted people to look up to me for all I do for the town. I'm not really a bad man."

Crudder had heard enough. With one quick movement, he drove the dagger home. *Only five more and Bandera will be free!*

The End

PREVIEW OF:

RETURN OF
MIDNIGHT MARAUDER
1872

BY ROY CLINTON

Chapter 1: Austin

I didn't set out to become the Midnight Marauder. When I accepted the fact my life was going to be that of a vigilante, I thought of myself as the Twilight Deliverer. But I guess Judge Gideon Anderson's last words to me about being a Midnight Marauder came closer to an accurate description of my role in life.

I'm John Crudder. In many ways, I feel like I have been somehow misplaced. I always seem to be out of my element. I live in the west but was raised in the east. Those I have been closest to in life are uneducated and some can neither read nor write. I have two degrees from Harvard, including one from Harvard Law School, and a Masters from Oxford.

My father was Robert Crudder, founder and builder of the Great National Railroad. I always suspected he had more money than God. When both he and my mother died in a buggy accident, I found out that I was not far off of the mark. He wanted me to follow in his footsteps and be a railroad executive. I tried but found my heart was just not in it. Instead, I sold his company and went to law school wanting to make a difference in the lives of people who would be denied justice without someone like me.

The thing I got from law school that stuck the most was the fact that the Scales of Justice must balance. For a while, I thought I could do that as an attorney. As I looked for a place to hang out my shingle, nothing captured my attention like the town of Bandera, Texas. I could have set up a practice in Bandera, for there was no competition. But I would have been idle most of the time because people simply didn't need a lawyer in Bandera—and if they did, they just rode a few miles to San Antonio and their legal needs were met.

Bandera gave me another opportunity that I never sought. I was appointed the town marshal, after I killed the murderer of their former marshal. As it turns out, just a few weeks into the job, I found out the town council was not only crooked, but all six were murderers. They were able to operate with impunity due to having several state officials on their payroll that would prevent anyone from seeking justice outside of Bandera.

I went to the telegraph office in Austin to see if I had gotten a message from my friends in Bandera. Sure enough I had. Listen to this cryptic message:

Aunt Mae, Austin, Texas

All is well here. Relax. Looking forward to seeing you again soon.

Slim and Charlotte

Previously, I had to leave Bandera in a hurry after dispatching the thoroughly corrupt judge. Oh, how I loved Bandera. I hurriedly wrote out a response to the telegram I had received.

Slim and Charlotte Hanson, Bandera, Texas

Have decided to return to Fort Worth for a while. Will write when I'm coming your way.

Aunt Mae

I sent the message and went outside to the hitching rail where my amazing stallion Midnight stood. The great horse whinnied when he saw me. I smiled at the silent communication that took place between the two of us. Midnight was ready to hit the trail.

I ducked under the hitching rail—not much of an effort since I just a little over five feet tall. Don't feel sorry for me. I came to peace with my short stature years before. Being short, I've had my share of bullies. But I have learned some effective skills at defending myself.

I untied the reins and mounted the tall horse as it turned in a circle and headed north. I held the thoroughbred to a trot until we cleared the last of Congress Avenue. When the last building slipped into the background, I relaxed my hold on the reins and Midnight immediately jumped into a full speed run.

No horse anywhere in the west could match Midnight's speed. With my small stature, the horse ran like it was on a racetrack with a jockey on board. I have never used spurs. Midnight naturally wanted to run as fast as I would allow. But he was also very responsive to my gentle touch on the reins and any time I shifted in the saddle.

I always laugh aloud when Midnight starts to run. Both horse and rider love to run and feel the wind. After about fifteen minutes, I slowed Midnight to a gentle lope and patted his neck. I'm in no hurry to get back to Fort Worth. What I need most is a long ride to contemplate my next move. I always think best when I'm atop Midnight riding across the countryside.

When it became obvious someone had to defend Bandera from the unholy six that comprised Bandera's town council, I had hoped that just eliminating the judge, who acted as the ring leader, would be enough to restore order. But deep down I knew there were five other evil people in Bandera who would continue to operate outside the reach of the law unless something or someone stopped them. I had wished there was some other way to restore justice to the Texas Hill Country town.

With cunning, stealth, and treachery, the council had targeted small landowners and pressured them to sell and leave town. For those who didn't respond to pressure, they ended up being buried in an unmarked graveyard outside of town. The council kept a troubleshooter or two in town to do their bidding. These tough cowboys blended in on ranches and carried out the orders of the council. The council would not hesitate to murder anyone who got in the way.

Chapter 2: Fort Worth

After about two weeks on the trail, I arrived in Fort Worth, went to the livery stable, and groomed Midnight. Then I went to the room I kept in the boarding house, took a bath and changed into a respectable suit, donned my derby hat and ivory inlaid cane and walked down the street to the haberdashery where I had previously been employed.

"Mr. Hamilton! I'm so glad to see you. When did you get back to town?"

"Mr. Asbury," I put on a thick British accent, just the way Asbury liked it. "Just call me Robert like you always have. I just got in about an hour ago. I thought I would see if my suits are ready for the final fitting."

"Indeed they are Mr., er, Robert," Asbury said as he went to the back room to retrieve my new tailor-made clothes. He didn't know my real name and never would. I used an alias to remain as anonymous as possible. "Sir, your shirts have also come in. As soon as you change, I'll begin the final fittings of each of your new suits. I have also just received some new swatches from London in case you want to order anything more."

I could hear the hopeful sound in Asbury's voice. "I believe I'm well fixed for now." Without intending to, I had disappointed Asbury. Not only am I a former employee, but I am the biggest customer he has ever had. "But I could use a new topcoat." Asbury immediately brightened.

"Robert, are you going to be coming back to work here?" Asbury asked hopefully. My privileged background gave me insight into knowing how to sell men's clothes to discriminating buyers. I had also convinced Asbury to begin offering a custom line of suits and shirts that were ordered from both New York City and London.

"I'm afraid I haven't time now," I responded as I looked at the fit of my suit in the mirror. "By the way, how are you doing with the new bespoke suits?"

"I must say that I'm amazed at how popular they are. I

never dreamed there would be so many men in this city who would want custom-tailored clothes—and be willing to pay a premium for the privilege."

"I'm glad to hear that, Mr. Asbury. You are providing a needed service for the city."

"Thanks to you, I don't think things could go any better."

When I reluctantly accepted my responsibility to deliver justice where it could not otherwise be found, I knew I needed an altered identity that would allow me to escape scrutiny. I easily fit into the role of an English gentleman. After finishing my first degree at Harvard, I had studied business at Oxford. Not wishing to continue to run my late father's railroad empire, I had sold my vast holdings, went back to Harvard, this time to law school, and then headed west.

I still haven't given up hope of someday living the ordinary life of a small-town lawyer, proposing to Charlotte, and maybe settling down in Bandera. But right now, that seems more of a dream than an achievable goal. Still, I choose to hold on to that hope.

CHAPTER 3: HUNTSVILLE

Texas had been readmitted to the Union two years ago, even though the state hadn't yet met all the requirements necessary for reentry. The Civil War had been over for some time and Texas had not seen much of the war action. I was not involved in the war because I was in college when the war started and well below the age of conscription. By the time I got back from graduate school in Great Brittan, the war was over.

I was shocked at the scars left in the aftermath of war. The loss of life was overwhelming. But the thing that bothered me the most was the nation was still deeply divided. As I headed west two years before, I was shocked to find most of the people I encountered continued to think of the south as being, if not at war, at least at odds with the rest of the nation.

From Fort Worth, I turned south with the thought of just exploring Texas with no particular destination in mind. After about two months, I arrived in Huntsville. I found the town friendly but also suffering from racial tension.

Reconstruction was difficult on Texas. In 1865, President Andrew Johnson appointed a Union General as provisional governor of Texas. Amnesty was granted to the ex-Confederates so long as they promised their loyalty to the Union. Before the war, thirty percent of the six hundred four thousand Texans were slaves. However, few in Texas would consider slaves true Texans since as slaves, they were thought to be less of a person than someone who was born free. With the end of the war and all former slaves freed, new tensions arose.

The Freedmen's Bureau was set up to help former slaves make the transition into free society and also to oversee labor contracts since they would now be paid wages under the free labor system. This was a federal program but the Freedmen's Bureau in Texas was very active in helping, at least on the surface, to make sure former slaves' rights were protected. However, it seemed more like another bureaucracy that was more concerned with the appearance of things rather than their true nature. It kept records of such things as the number of *murders and outrages* committed by *freedmen and white men*. They even kept records of the inspections of the Texas State Penitentiary in Huntsville and how the freedmen who were prisoners were being treated. According to reports, the prisoners were *well fed, well clothed,* and *kindly treated by the prison keepers* but there were many unofficial reports of continued mistreatment of the newly freed slaves. White supremacist groups were forming; there was a great deal of violence and intimidation toward black people in Texas.

Huntsville's economy, once being entirely based on cotton production, began to diversify. Lumber businesses began to grow and several sawmills were established. In 1871, the International and Great Southern Railroad came to Huntsville and helped spur lumber development. At least, it came near Huntsville.

The city fathers of Huntsville, in their esteemed wisdom, decided not to pay the bonus demanded by the railroad to get the tracks to run through the center of town. So, the railroad company simply laid their tracks bypassing

Huntsville. Faced with the extension of the community, the citizens of Huntsville went into an emergency fund-raising drive to raise money to build a spur from Huntsville to the main railroad. Huntsville residents raised ninety thousand dollars and the county contributed another thirty-five thousand dollars. Finally, the Huntsville Tap was built and connected Huntsville to the main railroad near the town of Phelps.

There are over one hundred plantations in Huntsville. Most are less than five hundred acres. Even with the lumber industry growing, cotton is still the main cash crop in central Texas and it depends heavily on slave labor. With the end of the Civil War, plantation owners are struggling to cope with the new reality of having to pay their former slaves for doing what they once did for free. Sixty percent of the people living in Walker County, Huntsville being the county seat, are black. Racial tensions have escalated.

One of the results of Reconstruction is the leasing of the state penitentiary to private individuals. These individuals pay the state for the convict labor and in turn, they are responsible for feeding and clothing the convicts and paying the guards. An outside camp system has developed where railroad companies and wealthy plantation owners hire convict labor and set up a labor camp near the railroad or on the grounds of a plantation. In one instance, a plantation owner is well known for brutalizing his labor force. Although there are guards present, they default to the supervisors of the plantation.

The Valdosta Plantation is the largest in Huntsville with over one thousand acres. Under orders from the plantation owner, those convicts, as well as the freedmen who didn't fill their daily cotton picking quota, are severely whipped. The whippings are so common that it was hardly noticed. I became aware of the mistreatment after visiting with the justice of the peace in Huntsville.

Using the practice I adopted in Fort Worth, I used an alias while in Huntsville. I continue to use Robert as my given name, since I'm accustomed to answering to it and because it is my late father's name. This time I used the surname of Johnson.

"So, Mr. Johnson," asked Justice of the Peace Oscar Simpson, "what's your business in Huntsville?"

"Well, first off, I need to find a job. Mainly I'm just drifting and looking for a place to settle down."

"You'll find Huntsville to your likin' all right." The justice looked at my worn boots and then lifted his eyes taking in every detail of my dress. "But I don't know about jobs. You see the colored folks take care of most of the plantation work. Besides that, you don't look like you're hankerin' to hoe any cotton. That's about all the work that's goin' on this time of year."

"You're shor right about that," I had to be conscious to use as much of a western twang as possible. After spending my formative years in New York and Boston, I have always been cognizant of using proper grammar and avoiding the idioms that are part of colloquial speech. In the two years I've been in the west, I have become more skilled at mimicking the speech patterns and inflection of the west. Sometimes I have found I can even think with a Texas drawl. But most of the time, I have had to make a conscious effort to sound more western.

"Don't know nothin' 'bout cotton. Much better acquainted with cattle and horses." I accepted Simpson's offer of coffee and a chair.

"Well, that puts a different light on things. Most of the plantations have a small cattle operation and some of them are hirin'. In fact, you might try the Valdosta Plantation just west of the Trinity River."

Simpson told how that plantation has a labor camp for

convicts from the Huntsville Penitentiary to work off their sentence. The labor camp and presence of the convicts makes it easier for the owner to discipline his own former slaves, now sharecroppers, in the same way. These poor souls don't know any different treatment and don't see any change since the war ended. Yes, they are told that they were free but they still feel like nothing had changed.

"Things are purty quiet 'round here now," Simpson continued. "But there weren't nothin' quiet a few months ago after Sam Jenkins got killed. "'Suspose you heard 'bout that?"

"Don't reckon I did. What happened?"

"Well, Jenkins was a freedman that was murdered. Weren't purty ah'tall. Cap McNeely hisself came down here to 'vestigate."

"Who?"

"Capt'n Leander H. McNeely of the Texas State Police. He's 'bout the best lawman in the state. He arrested four men for the murder. Three of them were found guilty. But then right there in the courtroom, all hell broke loose. Someone shot McNeely and some other lawman. All three men who had been found guilty escaped.

"But that weren't the end of it. Governor Davis

declared martial law. The militia came to town. Didn't think they'd ever leave. Must have stayed nigh onto two months. Claimed they never did find out who lynched ol' Jenkins. Weren't right. He's a darky and all, but nobody should be lynched."

I could feel the Scales of Justice in my head tilting badly. I know from experience that when that happens, I have to find a way to balance them. I thanked Simpson for the coffee and got directions to the Valdosta Plantation.

Ever since I was a child, I have found it difficult to watch people being treated unjustly. When I was a boy and tried to intervene, I got my butt whipped more often than not. But when I went to prep school at Georgetown in Washington DC, I joined the boxing team and learned some skills that would help me defend myself. After boxing practice, some of the older and larger team members taught me how to defend myself without the constraints of the rules imposed by formal boxing. Those skills have come in useful through the years.

I mounted Midnight and headed out following the directions the Justice of the Peace had given me. I didn't have to ride long before I came to a sprawling parcel of land covered with row after row of green plants that I guessed were cotton. I slowed Midnight to a walk and rode down the side of one large field. Each row had several black-skinned men and women with hoes chopping weeds. I listened and heard the workers singing in cadence.

Rounding one corner of the field, a man came riding toward me on horseback. "Can I help you?"

"Just rode out from town. Oscar Simpson said someone 'round here might be hirin'." I waited to see what kind of response I'd get. The rider looked me up and down. I knew from experience the man was probably thinking *what a little man to be ridin' such a big horse.*

"Well, might be hirin'. What kind of work you lookin' for?"

"I reckon I can do most anything—'cept chop cotton." I grin as I say it.

The rider smiled back. "Yeah, know whatcha mean. I guess you'll do. I'm Happy Jack. I'm foreman. If you can help with the cattle operation and some of the other things 'round here, you've got a job. That's 'long as you're not particular 'bout working with darkies, and you ain't 'specting to get rich."

"Name's Johnson. Robert Johnson. I reckon that sounds all right. When can I start?"

"Go on back to town and get the rest of your stuff. You can start when you get back."

"Don't have no more stuff." I tried to emulate the poor grammar of the foreman. "Just me an' my horse."

"You travel light. That's good. You can drop your bedroll and saddlebags at the bunkhouse behind the main house. There are two long buildin's where these folks live. The bunkhouse is much smaller. Don't think you'll have problems findin' it.

"Are these all former slaves?"

"You mean *freedmen*. That's what the law calls 'em now," Happy Jack replied. "'Bout half of 'em are *freedmen*. The other half are convicts. They're serving out their sentence here. Most of 'em ain't much trouble. But I do have to stay on 'em to make sure they work and don't slack off. Found a whip does a pretty good job of keepin' 'em in line."

I listened and took in what Happy Jack said.

"I'll head on to the bunkhouse. Where do I go after that?"

"Head south along the river. 'Bout a mile or two, you'll find the rest of the cowhands. They're moving the herd to the south most pasture. Just tell 'em I sent you."

I dropped off my bedroll and saddlebags at the

bunkhouse and headed down the river in search of the herd. Midnight adopted the easy lope he anticipated I wanted. I always smile as I think about my stallion's intelligence. It far surpasses that of some people I've known.

After about half of an hour, I came upon the herd. Riding up by one of the outriders I introduced myself.

"Name's Robert. Happy Jack just hired me."

"Name's Casey. Most call me One-Eyed Casey, 'cause I don't see so good in one eye. You go back and tell Wheeler to come on up. You're the new man. You ride drag."

"Suits me fine. Eatin' dust is my specialty."

I dropped back and found Wheeler who sure was happy to meet me. As he rode off I thought I'd made a great first impression on Wheeler. But I smiled to myself as I realized Wheeler was just happy to not be the last man on the drive.

As it turned out, riding drag wasn't so bad. There had been a shower earlier in the day so the cattle didn't kick up much dust. Truth be told, I like working by myself and listening to the cattle bawl. I also get to spend time with Midnight by myself. Midnight whinnies in response to me verbalizing my thoughts. I just kept riding and smiling.

About dusk, One-Eyed Casey called for all of us to bunch up the cattle for the night and make camp. Horses and cattle alike don't need much encouragement to stop and take a long drink of the silt-laden Trinity. While the water didn't look like much, it seemed the hands knew that it was clean and fresh.

I rode into camp and unsaddled Midnight. One of the hands already had a campfire going and a pot of beans hanging. I hadn't realized the small drive includes a chuck wagon. I accepted a plate of beans, a cold biscuit—no doubt left from breakfast—and a cup of coffee and took a seat with my upturned saddle to my back.

"Aren't you gonna hobble your horse?" Wheeler asked.

"Nope. Midnight will be right here in the morning. Horse has more sense than most people." Wheeler made introductions for me to the rest of the cowboys.

"This here's Robert. Happy Jack hired him today. You know One-Eyed. Then there's Pete and Justin."

"Howdy," I said and the other hands nodded in response.

Supper was pretty silent. Finally one of the hands said, "Wonder who's under the quirt tonight?"

"Don't matter. Those who don't get it tonight'll get it tomorrow night."

I'm not sure which hand said that, but as I listened, I

learned more about how Happy Jack got the production he needed on the cotton plantation. It seems Happy Jack is happiest when he is doling out punishment to the prisoners and the former slaves. I found out Happy Jack was a sergeant in the Confederacy. He hadn't taken well to the thought that slaves had to be freed. But he certainly seemed to enjoy being able to use his power to keep all of the plantation hands in line.

When the sun came up, the cowboys were already saddled up and ready to ride as soon as breakfast was over. To my happy surprise, there were fresh biscuits and bacon and some of the best coffee I've ever had. None of the hands seemed to find the breakfast out of the ordinary. I kept my opinion to myself. Above all else, I didn't want to stand out.

We mounted up and drove the cattle through the day down to just north of Madisonville. When evening came, we made camp by a small lake. The chuck wagon was already set up and the beans were hot. I smelled the coffee and remembered how much I enjoyed it at breakfast. This time the coffee had a burnt taste. I realized the cook is serving leftover coffee to go with the leftover beans and biscuits.

I put my back to my upturned saddle and tasted the

beans. For a brief moment, I had a flash of memory of the wonderful meals my childhood nanny, Alvelda, had cooked for me. I also couldn't help but think of the world-class fare I regularly ate in New York, Boston, and London. In spite of being raised with wealth and privilege, I don't miss that lifestyle. I feel at home in the west.

That evening I spent time with Wheeler talking about a variety of things including Happy Jack's propensity for violence.

"Things got a bit tense around here late last year. Sam Jenkins worked here. He used to be a slave here and was always making trouble for Happy Jack—'till Jack killed him. Seems he felt his *freedman status* gave him some special privilege. There was never a week when Sam was whipped with a quirt less than three times. Sometimes it happened every day."

"How can anyone survive that kind of treatment?"

"Well that's the thing. Each day he got weaker and weaker. He first got the quirt because he missed his picking quota. Then the next day he missed it worse. Happy Jack thought he was doing it on purpose—just trying to show 'em he was right."

"So what happened?"

"Happy Jack just kept whippin' Sam. Every time he did, he just smiled like he was especially enjoying it. That's why he's called Happy Jack. You'll see for yourself one of these days. Jack likes to put on a show when he's whippin' someone, freedman or convict."

I feel the Scales of Justice swing wildly as I listen to Wheeler. How could someone get away with murder and then brag about it? It seems I kept running into people who are able to live above the law and remain untouchable.

"I never heard of a quirt before."

"That's Meskin for whip." Wheeler continued telling his story. "Anyway, even as weak as he was, Sam would stand and take it. Jack couldn't break him. He started talking crazy about taking Sam out and lynchin' him. We said we didn't want no part of it. But the next night, shor nuff, ol' Sam got strung up right down on the river 'bout a half mile from the bunkhouse. Hung him from an old sycamore that's got a low hangin' limb."

"So did Happy Jack kill him?"

"No doubt 'bout it. Jack was even arrested by Capt'n McNeely 'long with three other hands from the plantation. Jack was the only one not convicted. But 'fore the judge could announce the sentence, there was shootin' in the courtroom. Capt'n got shot. So did another lawman standin' round. No one knew where the guns came from but all four who were on trial had one as well as many of the men a-watchin'. The three who were found guilty rode out of town. Ain't been seen 'round here since."

"So if Jack was found not guilty, why do you think he did it?"

"Everybody knows Happy Jack done it," Wheeler continued. "He even bragged 'bout it. They just never had any evidence to convict him. Then after he got off, they say he can't be tried again so it don't matter him sayin' he done it."

"It's called double jeopardy.

"Double what?"

"Oh nothin'. Just means that a person can't be tried again after he's been found not guilty."

"Don't seem right to me."

After supper, I tried going to sleep, but just kept hearing the words of Wheeler and how Happy Jack lived above the law and bragged about it. The worst part is that the law can't do anything about it.

This is where I have a real battle going on inside. I don't think I have been appointed by God to see that justice is served. But I do believe someone has to stand up for those who don't have the protection of the law. Ever since I first saw the Scales of Justice in law school, it's as though the scales are in my head and as long as they are out of balance, I am not able to rest.

Just before sunrise, I woke up thinking about Sam Jenkins getting hung for being proud and defiant. Neither thing is a crime. I was not sure when I would have a chance to see justice served and Happy Jack pay for his crime.

Shortly before sunrise, One-Eyed Casey woke up the hands.

"Better get up. If we're gonna make the plantation by dusk we better get ridin'. I sent the chuck wagon on ahead after supper last night. The cook's mules know the way back home and Cookie'll sleep in the back like a baby. Prob'ly beat us home."

And with those words, all of us saddled up and took some day-old biscuits for our saddlebags. I mounted Midnight and got the feeling my handsome steed would love to challenge the rest of the horses to a race. I laughed at the thought of the spectacle that would make. I held the reins taut for a few minutes until Midnight realized he needed to lope with the other horses. I could tell the stallion doesn't like being around more ordinary horses.

I rode quietly through the day contemplating what I had learned about Happy Jack. The time will come when I will see that justice comes to Huntsville. Little did I know that the time was coming sooner than I imagined.

That evening back at the plantation, I was treated to my first meal on the large spread. There was a small dining hall, just big enough for the cowhands and others that work for Happy Jack. The freedmen and convicts are fed in the yard where they sat on the ground and ate with their hands since none are afforded the privilege of using a fork or a spoon.

When I come out of the dining hall, I heard some of the cowboys yelling like they were rooting for someone to win a fight. What I see instead is Happy Jack violently whipping one of the former slaves. The man was tied across a barrel with his naked back exposed. With each lash, I saw Jack smile to the point of laughing.

I lunged forward to stop the violent beating but Wheeler stepped in quickly and pulled me back.

"You best not git mixed up in that. Happy Jack'll turn on you. He'll give you worse than he's givin' that darky.

A noticeably pregnant woman rushed up to Happy Jack and grabbed his whip hand. Jack shook her off and she fell at his feet. I watched in horror as Jack pulled back his leg and kicked her hard in her swollen stomach.

"Let that be a lesson to all you darkies. You mess with Happy Jack, you're gonna pay the price. You don't do your work, you're gonna pay. You cause any trouble ah'tal, you will pay. Anybody else want some of this?" Jack lifted the quirt into the air and let it fall one more time on the back of the nearly unconscious man.

When Wheeler released his hold on me, I was shaking with anger. I was sick to my stomach with what I have seen. I would not have believed it possible that one human being could do that to another human being if I had not seen it with my own eyes.

I walked a few yards away and vomited up my supper. My stomach continued to heave until there was nothing else to retch up. It was this moment when I knew I couldn't work there anymore. I also knew that I was going to have to be the one to make the Scales of Justice balance.

The next morning, I heard the pregnant woman who was kicked by Happy Jack prematurely delivered her baby who was born dead—no doubt the result if Jack's vicious kick in her stomach. Oh how I wanted to see Jack pay for what he had done.

"I'm quittin' and ridin' on," I told Wheeler. "There's too much killin' 'round here for me."

"Don't blame you none. I prob'ly won't be far behind you. I've 'bout had nuff of this place, too."

I saddled Midnight, then mounted my great horse. I turned to Wheeler and just shook my head in disgust at what I'd witnessed.

"Ain't you gonna draw your pay?" asked Wheeler.

"I don't want no part of money from a place like this." I turned my horse south and allowed Midnight to take on a fast lope. In a few minutes, I slowed to a walk as I approached the river. I pulled up at the base of the great sycamore where Happy Jack lynched Sam Jenkins. Looking at the tree, I could envision Jenkins swinging from the low hanging limb.

Slowly, I rode on by, crossing the Trinity River and continuing south. I would find a place to wait for the right time to rebalance the Scales of Justice. Right then, all I could do was wait.

After two weeks of eating squirrels I'd shot, I knew I needed to go into town to get supplies. I turned back toward Huntsville. About thirteen miles out of town, I got to a general store in the community that had sprung up around the railroad stop called Waverly Station. I bought the usual: bacon, flour, coffee, salt, baking powder, a little sugar, and a box of cartridges for my six-gun and another for my saddle gun.

That night I made camp just outside of Waverly and made myself a supper of biscuits, coffee, and bacon I roasted on a stick. I was getting the feeling that would be the night for me to settle things with Happy Jack. What I didn't know was how I was going to get Jack out of the bunkhouse without making a disturbance.

As I rode into the compound of bunkhouses, everything is quiet and dark. That is, all except the bunkhouse where the freedmen live. I tied Midnight outside the compound and silently slipped up to the door of the bunkhouse. Inside, I could hear the breathing of many people and soft whispers. I crept into the door and stepped into the shadows. I found it difficult to believe what I was seeing.

The former slaves had Jack stripped naked. His hands were tied behind him and his feet were tied. A rag was stuffed in his mouth. One by one, the former slaves who had been so abused by Jack took the quirt that had abused them and administered several hard lashes with all of their strength. Then they regained their composure and passed the quirt to the next person who did the same. I was struck at how silent and composed the rest of the group was as Jack received his whipping. If not for the whipping taking place, it was as though the assembled freedmen are in church.

After several minutes, I stepped from the shadows. There was a collective gasp from the assembled group. I put a finger to my lips to calm them.

"Please don't be afraid. I didn't come to stop you. This man deserves all you have done and more. I don't want to interrupt you. But when you're done, Happy Jack has more to answer for."

"He came in here to take away another of our women," cried an old man. "He does that every week. He just comes and takes what he wants and no one can stop him."

"I saw you that night when he kicked and killed my baby. You tried to stop him but other men held you."

"Yes, I saw him kill your baby. He has to pay for that. And he also had to pay for killin' Sam Jenkins. When you're finished with him, I intend to give him what he has comin'."

The group silently nodded in unison.

"You take him Mister. What do we say when we're asked who took him?"

"Tell him the Midnight Marauder came and took him while he was here trying to abuse your women."

End of Preview

Read the next adventure of John Crudder in

Return of Midnight Marauder

Order now at:

www.TopWesterns.com

www.Amazon.com

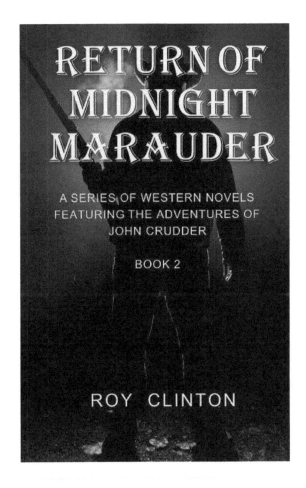

ACKNOWLEDGMENTS

First I would like to thank my wife Kathie for her encouragement. She willingly gave up part of a vacation so we could do research in New York City about the church, cemetery, and plaque on the pew (yes, it is there exactly as written except with a different name) descried in this book. She has also encouraged me as I have gone on numerous writing retreats. Kathie, I love you.

Recently, I have become acquainted with prolific Western author Paul L. Thompson. I was shocked when Paul called me early one morning and told me he got up at four o'clock that morning and started reading the manuscript I had sent him. His words of encouragement made me feel like I had just written the next bestseller. He asked me if I minded if he did some editing on the manuscript. *Mind? How could I mind? Of course, I would be honored to have the best-selling Western novelist* (more than thirty novels) *edit my work.* Paul gave me a crash course in Western novel writing, made wonderful suggestions on the manuscript ("I removed the word 'that' eighty-one times"), and gave me a spelling lesson for Western dialogue. While I knew cowboys didn't say "sure," I also found out they don't say "shore." ("Just drop the e. It's shor.") Well Paul, I shor 'preciate your help.

I would like to thank Sharon Smith of Akron, Ohio, for her wonderful proofreading. She has proofed at least four of my books. Any mistakes you find in the manuscript are due solely to me making additions after her corrections. Sharon, you are an indispensable part of my team.

I would also like to thank Teresa Lauer who has devoted many hours to making sure this book gets into production. She has designed the cover as well as having done the overall book design. Teresa, I appreciate your knack of making my ideas become reality.

I have sought to be historically accurate as to events and places. For example, the name of the pastor of Trinity

Church, details about the history of the church, who is buried in the cemetery that adjoins it, the name of the degree awarded at Harvard, the vessel John used to get to Europe, as well as the historically significant details like conscription in the Civil War. I did take some liberty with the details of the death of Sam Jenkins but the trial, the name of the governor in Texas at the time, and the mood of the state are all historically correct.

I'm always glad to hear from readers. You may reach me at Roy@TopWesterns.com. It may be few days before I respond but I will respond to every email.

I need your HELP!!
Willing to write a review on Amazon?

Here's how :
1) go to amazon.com
2) search for Roy Clinton
3) click on appropriate title
4) write a review

The review you write will help get the word out to others who may benefit.

— Thanks for your help,
Roy Clinton